THE
INHERITANCE

THE INHERITANCE

PAUL PETERS

TESTIMONIALS

"*The Inheritance* reminded me that the most meaningful success isn't measured in accolades or wealth, but in the strength of our character, and the people whose lives we quietly influence. I appreciated how the story gives space to struggle without glorifying it, while showing how purpose often emerges slowly, through perseverance and faith in something larger than ourselves. What stayed with me was the sense of legacy: not as something handed down, but as something earned through service, sacrifice, and love. It's a powerful reminder that our lives matter most when they create opportunity, and hope for others, especially the generations that will follow."

– David Trent, Founder and CEO of TrentSuccess

"The Inheritance...this book had me at 'hello!' This book not only captured my attention, it demanded my attention! You will not be easily distracted from this, so I recommend you put the book out of sight during dinner time with your friends or family. The character, 'Jacob' was a man who was clearly not a quitter! The vivid descriptions made it easy to imagine it was happening in 3D right in front of you! 'The Inheritance' has a sweet spot for any audience. If I were a school teacher I would make this a mandatory read for my students."

–Kim Wood, Customer Clothier Pearce Bespoke

"<u>The Inheritance </u>is a timeless quest for fulfillment and purpose. Through Jacob's chosen and redirected paths, he discovers what truly matters, and finds his deepest purpose. His journey (blessed by success, tempered by burden) leads to a serene, meaningful ending. This book invites you to seek your own destined purpose, and to share that happiness with those you love, remembering that every joy may bear a cost."

-Susie Juneau

THE INHERITANCE

Paul Peters

Copyright © 2026

All rights reserved.

ISBN: 978-1-968149-15-4

Joint Venture Publishing

The Millionaire Mentor, Inc.

TABLE OF CONTENTS

INTRODUCTION

FOREWORD

About the Author

FOREWORD BY GREG REID

Every so often, a book comes along that doesn't simply entertain–it awakens something in us. *The Inheritance* by Paul Peters is one of those rare works that carries with it a heartbeat, a pulse, a truth that reaches beyond its pages and settles into the soul of the reader. Jacob's journey is more than a compelling narrative of struggle, redemption, and triumph–it's a parable that mirrors the path walked by its author. Though told through fiction, Jacob's battles with loss, identity, faith, and purpose reflect the lived experience of a man who has traveled through his own valleys, leaned on grace, and emerged with a calling to serve.

Paul Peters has penned a book about overcoming adversity not by sheer will alone, but by surrendering to the transformative force of faith, it is a book about discovering purpose not in achievements, but in compassion and giving. And, undeniably, it is a love story–between a man and his God, a man and his family, and ultimately a man learning to love his own reflection after years spent running from it. Jacob's life reminds us that legacy is not defined by wealth, but by character, courage, and the lives we touch. His story will challenge you to look inward and ask: *What am I meant to leave behind? What will be my inheritance to the world?*

–Greg Reid, #1 Best-Selling author, founder of Secret Knock

INTRODUCTION

After writing my first book, "Discovering and Embracing your Life Purpose," as a nonfiction "how to" book on helping people to discover their purpose, I wanted to put the much-needed discovery into a fictional book to tell the story of Jake Steel, who was on a quest to find his "purpose," and to then share it with others to serve. The idea of this book has come about over many years of pursuing the truth and discovery of principles that I have tried to apply in my life.

After the publication of my first book, came my second book "Ways of Wisdom," in 2022. My latest book "Success Redefined," which I co-authored with Jack Canfield, was released in 2024 and immediately became a best seller on day one! "The Inheritance," is my fourth book project, and it details within a fictional story, how one man discovered his purpose throughout many trials, while building an empire that impacted a world, and left a legacy that would prove to have a direct and lasting impact on his grandkids, as well as generation upon generation thereafter.

As we go through the life story of Jake, beginning in 1925, we will go into much detail on "the pieces of the puzzle" he had to discover that, once put together, would make the picture clearer for him. I will provide the details of Jake's life from 1925 to 2015 and all he went through to find his purpose. While demonstrating how most of us may find our purpose if we are willing to see and understand the clues or puzzle pieces left for us.

It is my hope this book will bring you one step closer in the discovery of who you are, and why you are here. It is a deep question that has plagued countless people throughout time. The very asking, spurs the process of discovery. In the searching comes the discovery. In the discovery comes the meaning and fulfillment of one's life.

CHAPTER

1

"The Beginning Years"

It's the summer of 1925 in Stoney Point, a small rural farm town with no more than 700 inhabitants. Daylight lasts longer now, which means days begin at the crack of dawn in order to avoid the midday heat. It's 9:00 am and the typical sounds of hustle and bustle are stirring in the home of Abraham and Sara Steele, where most of their 9 kids have already been up for several hours, doing their chores and rustling up some lunch. August 23rd, is the day they will welcome their 10th and final child. Sara's labor pains begin as she leaves the kitchen to find a place to rest. Abraham and the kids offer her help as they each do their part to see that their mother is comfortable. While they are not sure if they will be blessed with a boy or girl, names have been picked out for either. It is no secret they are hoping for a boy who they'll name Jacob. However, a healthy baby is what they truly are praying for, and if God should honor them with a girl, then she will be named Abigail.

When Sara's water breaks, she yells for her oldest child, Jenny, to go get Papa and let him know she is about to give birth to their child. Jenny swiftly runs out to the fields where Papa is on his tractor working. She screams, "Papa, come quickly!" Papa directs Jenny to run and fetch Mrs. McDougall as fast as she can to help with the delivery. Papa arrives as Mama is screaming in pain, and although he has experienced this process nine times before, he still feels a bit helpless as he can offer no immediate relief to his wife's pain and discomfort. Shortly thereafter, Mrs. McDougall, like a drill sergeant, barks orders to get Papa out of the house and instructs Bessie Ann to take care of the kids. Mrs. McDougall calms Sara down and begins to assist her with the delivery of the little baby. The labor goes into its 12th hour, and the pushing has left Sara exhausted. Mrs. McDougall recognizes that the baby is in the breach position and immediately yells for Bessie Ann to round up the kids and start praying. As Mrs. McDougall prays out loud, and as she reaches in to turn the little baby, she notices that little Jacob's head is coming out. This whole time Abraham is pacing outside praying for his Sara and their little baby boy. With feelings of exhaustion and relief, both Mrs. McDougall and Sara cry, praising God for this newborn miracle. At 10:02 p.m. the Lord has blessed them with little baby Jacob, and Mrs. McDougall proudly proclaims to the others, "It's a boy!" Placing him in Sara's arms, she begins the post-delivery process of cutting the umbilical cord and checking the vitals of both the mother and baby. Abraham and the kids hear the baby's cries and crowd around to celebrate the newest member of the Steele family. Papa falls to his knees and weeps, thanking God for their new baby boy. When they all rush into the house to see Mama and little Jacob, Mrs. McDougall directs everyone to wait patiently and give Mama and baby some space. She does, however, allow Papa to come in and share a moment with Mama and little Jacob, and weeping together, they hold their miracle baby. After weighing Jacob, Mrs. McDougall announces he weighs 9 pounds 7 ounces, and with her deep Irish accent exclaims, "This here chap is a biggin!"

After caring for Sara and Jacob for a few days, she reaches out to the local doctor who makes a house call to check on Sara and her child. Doctor Carson had been the physician for all of their children, and after examining Jacob, he informed Sara and Abraham that due to the baby's breach position, issues with turning, and the umbilical cord being wrapped around him, with limited oxygen, it was a miracle he was a healthy baby boy. This official news from the doctor was a relief and blessing, and soon after his clean bill of health, life began to settle back to normal for the Steele family; Mrs. McDougall and Bessie Ann helped out with Sara, Jacob, and the other children, who while still young, all had chores to do. The girls were responsible for helping Mama with the housework and taking care of laundry and cleaning. At the ripe old age of 10, Jenny, the oldest and Mama's big helper, had been endearingly nicknamed by her brothers and sisters as "Boss Lady." Amazingly organized, she directed most of the kids with their daily duties. Mama depended on her, especially now that she had Jake and Gary, who was only two years old. Jenny helped organize Luis and Lane, the twins who were 8 and the hellions of the family, as they were always fighting and shared a free-spiritedness that tested Papa's patience at times. He had the belt ready for those two each day as they had the rebellious spirit in them from day one. They had the responsibility to care for feeding the farm animals and cleaning their stalls. The Steele family had horses, mules, pigs, chickens and cows, so there was always something that needed to be done around their farm. Mark and Keith, who were 7 and 6, also had to help. Their main jobs were to gather the chickens and milk the cows. The kids' day started at 5.00 a.m. with their chores, which they completed before they went off to school at 8. Things were a bit crazy in the morning with making sure everyone was up, fed, and had their chores finished on time, but it became a solid routine that ran like clockwork.

The kids had to catch the horse-drawn school carriage that picked them up nearby. At the time of Jake's birth, Jenny, Scarlet, Luis, Lane, Mark, Keith, and Lauren were all attending elementary school. The schoolhouse was small, and all the children were in the same room. They had a wonderful teacher named Ms. Hannah Goodchild, who was only 23 and new to the school. She loved the children and had such a youthful imagination and the kids felt at ease relating to her. Ms. Goodchild was such a great role model to the children and always encouraged them to believe in themselves and never stop pursuing their dreams. Ms. Goodchild's dream had always been to be a teacher and she was naturally gifted at creating lessons and lesson plans that were very easy for kids to comprehend. She was particularly gifted at weaving each lesson into stories that helped the students understand at their level. She was also amazingly patient, while still maintaining a firm, but gentle approach. She was even able to tame Luis and Lane, who never gave her any problems or showed her any disrespect. Some would even say she was an angel in disguise, given her natural giftedness with kids. She would later make a huge impression on Jake as he entered school and would forever leave an indelible mark on him that lasted his entire life. Overall, Ms. Goodchild had about 30 kids to teach, and the number kept growing. Her favorite subject to teach was history because the stories of old would captivate the kids and stoke their imagination.

For the first few years, life seemed to be going well as the family settled into a nice daily routine. They had always been a close-knit family that was active in church. Mama made sure she prayed with each of the kids before bed and encouraged them to always be there for one another. Always speaking kind and encouraging words to them, she reminded each of them that they were very special and valuable. "Each of you were created in God's image, and He has a special calling for you in this life," she would say to them. This especially resonated with Jake, and as he grew older, he reflected on the love and faith within her words. His mama laid a foundation for his faith that he'd never forget, as it would serve as a life-saving force when he needed it most.

Then in 1929, disaster struck across America with the onset of the Great Depression and the crash of Wall Street. It greatly affected Papa soon thereafter with his inability to make ends meet and provide for his family. Jake was turning five at that time and was just entering school. About a year and a half later, their situation worsened when Mama came down with Scarlet Fever and became bedridden for over a year. Each of the kids had to pitch in even more and Jenny had to quit school at 16 to tend to Mama while her siblings were in school. After the kids came home from school, she went to work selling eggs and working as a housekeeper/nanny to the Smiths, a well-to-do family in the community. When she was working, Scarlet replaced Jenny with helping Mama. Luis and Lane, who were now 13, had to pick up the slack on the farm so there would be food on the table. In the meantime, Mark and Keith contributed too, by taking odd jobs whenever they could to make extra money. Lauren and Susie took on the majority of the work hours with cooking and cleaning. It was a strain on the family, especially with Mama's health issues, and the medical bills that were piling up. Ms. Goodchild was a major help during this trying time and could be counted on to tutor and work with Jenny so she wouldn't fall behind in her schoolwork. Jake loved Ms. Goodchild and treated her much like a second mother. They had no idea at the time what an impact she would have on each of them throughout their lives.

A few years later, when Jake was 9, Mama took ill from the cold weather. The Scarlet Fever weakened her health and made her more susceptible to sickness. Sadly, she wouldn't survive through the winter, and on December 28, 1934, three days after they spent their last Christmas together, their beloved Mama passed away. At the time, Jenny was 19, Scarlet 18, Lane and Luis 17, Mark 16, Keith 15, Lauren 14, Susie 13, Gary 11, and Jake 9. It was a very sad time for the Steele family as Mama had always been their rock, and now she was gone. Papa was grief-stricken and took to drinking. He knew things were bad and had been for quite some time, and had relied on his kids, especially the older ones, during Mama's illness. By then Ms. Goodchild had become a part of the family; not only was she fond of them, but she couldn't forget the conversation when Mama asked her to watch over her children.

With Mama's absence and Papa's drinking, the next few years were especially hard for everyone. Jenny and Scarlet both married their long-time boyfriends and moved away. Luis and Lane were always fighting with Papa, and they eventually moved out, got jobs at the mill, and later joined the Army. Mark and Keith soon enlisted in the Air Force, while Lauren was finishing up high school with plans on attending nursing school thereafter. With their older siblings gone, Susie, Gary, and Jake were the only children left at home. Susie took care of all the housework and cooking, while Gary and Jake were left to tend to the farm. The saving grace around their home was Ms. Goodchild, who helped mentor and raise the remaining children. She also protected the kids from Papa, who was struggling with the bottle and flying off the handle in fits of rage. Ms. Goodchild was a natural peacemaker and knew what to do and say in order to diffuse most of his temper tantrums; however, there were times when Papa's temper would get the best of him. When Jake was around 13, Ms. Goodchild and Papa ended up getting married. This proved to be life-changing for Jake, who saw her as a second mother and a very strong role-model and mentor. She spent every day with Jake, Susie, and Gary making sure to pray with and tutor them on the important things in life. She was an amazing story-teller and would keep the kids spellbound for hours while weaving stories of adventure.

From the ages of 5 through 17, Ms. Goodchild played a vital role in Jake's life, especially after his mother's illness and eventual death and his father's pressures and struggles. Jake would later reflect on how he became conflicted over faith after all the tragedy he and his family endured. When he was younger, he blamed God for all their heartache and grief. This resulted in confusion since he also believed it was God who brought Ms. Goodchild into their lives.

Susie soon began college and because it had become increasingly difficult to be around Papa due to his bad temper, she moved out. So it was now just Papa, Ms. Goodchild, Gary, and Jake remaining in the Steele home. Papa was not doing well on the farm as bills were piling up and stress was mounting. More pressure was placed on Gary and Jake to fill in as Papa's drinking problems worsened. It got so bad that even Ms. Goodchild could not reason with him, and he was becoming increasingly erratic. One day when Jake turned 16 and was returning home from school, he began his usual routine of handling his daily chores but something seemed off, so he went searching for Papa, but there was no reply when he yelled for him. He searched the house and called for Gary, but to no avail as he was busy working in the fields while Ms. Goodchild was tending to the housework. As it grew, dark they became worried about Papa's whereabouts. Jake looked around and came upon an opened envelope next to Papa's chair and decided to take a look. The blood drained from his face when he saw a letter from the bank addressed to Abraham Steele, stating they would be taking over the farm soon due to non-payment. They would be expected to vacate the property within 30 days or payoff the balance of what was owed. After not being able to find Ms. Goodchild who had stepped out to get milk. Jake rushed to the barn frantically looking for Papa, where he heard an eerie noise, as if something was hitting the barn door. It was already dark so it was hard for him to see, but what he could make out was a shadow, cast by the light of the moon, and it was Papa who was hanging from a rope. Jake screamed for Gary as he ran to loosen the rope around his father's neck, but it was too late. Papa was gone! Jake wept over Papa as he held his lifeless body in his arms. He cursed God, questioning how God could take Mama, and now Papa from their family. That was how Ms. Goodchild and Gary found him when they ran into the barn. In absolute shock at what had happened, they surrounded Papa and wept together.

The next few days were a whirlwind of emotion as news spread like wildfire and the family rallied around to support one another. Both Jenny and Scarlet arrived with their respective two-year-old children and Luis, Lane. Keith, and Mark, all took a leave from military service to attend the funeral and be with their family. Lauren and Susie also took a break from school to join them. Once again, the Steele family was together, minus Mama and Papa, but this time they came together to console each other, while the warm-hearted Ms. Goodchild held their hands and prayed with them. Jake, who witnessed firsthand the horror of seeing Papa hanging, was having the worst time dealing with his death as it was a sad reminder of having lost both parents. For some reason, he blamed himself for not only his mother's death, but also his father's. He felt that perhaps if he hadn't been born, they wouldn't have had to endure such a hard life. He also blamed God.

CHAPTER

2

"A Call to War"

It was a chilly December afternoon in 1941, and Jacob was on his break at the mill. Ms. Goodchild had packed him a fried egg sandwich, sliced carrots, nuts, dried fruit, and a wedge of cake she made the day before, along with a thermos of black coffee. As he ate and gazed at the valley below, he took a deep breath and digested the majestic view. There was a smattering of freshly fallen snow in town, and he was momentarily mesmerized at the view. He usually loved this time of year as Christmas approached. However, the holiday season wouldn't be the same without his Mama and Papa as well all his siblings that used to gather around their farmhouse hearth while singing Christmas songs. Those were memories he cherished, as life was simpler back when the Steele family enjoyed comfortable times.

He tried best he could to dispel the memories of Mama lying in bed, weak from her illnesses, then her eventual and untimely death. But he couldn't help his mind from drawing upon those times, too. It seemed the more he told himself not to think of those horrible moments in his life, the more they appeared in his head. Papa's ensuing drinking and belligerency reminded Jake how life could take a turn in a moment, and the fallout that follows when people are under duress. It was a vicious cycle of events that seemed to perpetuate the next; had Mama not gotten ill and died, then Papa wouldn't have fallen to drinking, and if the Great Depression hadn't occurred, the pressures wouldn't have changed the entire dynamic of a once simple and happy life. Jake pondered these scenarios often, but the reality of it all was these things unfortunately did happen, and the realization was that good things happen to good people all the time. Like Ms Goodchild reminded him over and over again, "It's not always what happens to you that's the most impactful thing, but how you respond to those events truly is the test of your character." Still, he held on to the guilt, as he wondered if his family would have been better off without him.

Ms. Goodchild included a note in his lunchbox, as she was prone to do once in a while. This particular note was a quote from Walt Whitman that read, "Keep your face always toward the sunshine—and shadows will fall behind you." As Jake processed his interpretation of the note, he slightly exhaled with a gasp, as Ms. Goodchild's usual impeccable timing with words of wisdom was present in his life at the right moment once again. The moral of the note was a reminder to look at the good, the positive, the light, and that stance will ensure the past darkness is left behind. These words certainly distracted him from the gloomy thoughts that were seeping through his head at that moment.

Ms. Goodchild became more than a teacher and stepmother to Jake these days, as she was a mentor of sorts now. Possibly out of necessity, she realized Jake emitted a tough exterior pose, deep down inside, he was still a sensitive boy, who experienced trauma that no child should ever be forced to deal with. She was his savior in many ways, and Jake recalled those deep conversations with Mama as she lay dying, reminding him to listen to Ms. Goodchild, and she would guide him.

After Jacob finished his lunch, he grabbed his gloves and returned inside the vast mill. It was a loud bustling place filled with machines churning and people hard at work. It was hard to hear a conversation, which management preferred so workers would be less distracted. Jake didn't love the work, but was grateful to be employed and earning an honest wage, and he took pride in his job, as he always put forth his very best effort into each task at hand. He had developed a natural drive, and when he put his mind to something, it was near impossible for someone to change it. At seventeen years old, he possessed a maturity and mindset of someone much older. He seemed familiar with whatever topic of conversation surrounded him and felt very comfortable interjecting and adding to such discussions. However, Jake steered clear of small talk and gossip as he considered it a waste of time and spoken by small-minded people. He had higher hopes than life in a small town and/or working at a mill in a laborious role. He hadn't quite honed in on his particular career path, but knew it would be in an entrepreneurial role.

The chaotic sounds of the mill suddenly ceased and one could now hear a pin drop within the factory as machines came to a halt. Jake's first thought was someone suffered an injury with one of the machines, or had a heart attack, which had already happened a few times since he began working there. This was different, as the eerie silence was broken by the whispers of the shop lead and supervisor, who were having a very serious conversation that piqued the curiosity of the onlookers. The bell sounded prematurely as it was four hours early from their shift ending. Workers stood dumbfounded as echoes of chit chat could be heard throughout the vast warehouse. Finally, over the loud speaker there was an announcement, "America was attacked at Pearl Harbor today as Japanese planes invaded U.S. air space and bombed the naval base in Honolulu, Hawaii. Reports are still coming in with regard to the casualties, and what this all means will soon follow. Take ten minutes paid time and gather yourselves, then back to work."

Whispers turned into full-fledged conversations as everybody wondered what was next for America, as it had steered clear of engagement to this point. But this move by the Japanese would require retaliation and eventual involvement in World War II. Jake, whose brothers were in the military, immediately wondered what this would mean for them. He said a silent prayer for the safety of his family and country. As his coworkers theorized, Jake's thoughts about his future career path and his current employment would be put on hold, as he decided right there and then he would enlist.

On December 8, 1941 Franklin Delano Roosevelt delivered his "Day of Infamy Speech" to a joint session of Congress as he expressed outrage at Japan and its attack on Pearl Harbor. Within 72 hours, the United States of America's declared war and full involvement within World War II.

As a seventeen year old, Jake had devised a plan before he entered the doors of the local recruitment office, to add one more year to his age so he could join forces in the fight. Within a couple hours, Jacob Steele was an official member of the United States Navy and hell bent on fighting for the very country he was a proud citizen of. There was no apprehension or question about his decision, as he knew it was a noble and worthy cause. When backed by what he believed in, Jake was an unstoppable force, as he had developed a high sense of integrity and loyalty through his parents' teachings. Ms. Goodchild, too, was an integral part of Jake's growth with regard to the pursuit of doing what's right. However, she had reservations for young Jake and made it clear that although she was fervently against violence and war, she, too, knew that the future of their country and its freedom was at stake, and although deeply concerned for his and his brother's safety, Ms. Goodchild was proud of his decision and his belief behind it.

Many a conversations took place between the two, as they discussed and prayed on the issue at hand, and she asked God to guide the boy that she had come to consider a son. Ms. Goodchild also spent evenings on her knees talking with his late mother, through her prayers, to help her provide the proper advice to pass along to her son, in addition to well wishes for her other boys who were also in the fight. This was a precarious time in the country as they were provoked into a war which they had previously held a neutral stance. Towns across America had joined forces as employees and factories worked tirelessly to produce the goods needed to support their young countrymen. It was a time of full involvement and engagement as the citizens of the United States of America held its proverbial breath in the face of the unknown. Other countries too had come to rely on the bravery and resolve of the U.S. to help the cause, thus placing even more pressure on the country to fight the good fight.

Within weeks, young Jake was given his deployment orders and was now a full-fledged member of the United States Navy. He felt a passionate patriotic duty to serve his country by becoming a sailor with the desire to fight against the Japanese and German forces, as well as anybody who threatened the freedom and safety of America. Many young American men were urged to join the military in the early 1940's, but now most of them needed no more provoking than that of the Pearl Harbor attacks. Jacob felt both a sense of relief and anxiousness as he boarded the majestic ship that he'd call home for the next several years. His sense of direction had been chosen for him in a way, and that brought a strong feeling of purpose to him. He knew what he needed to do and where he needed to be. In his eyes, the other chapters of his journey would fall in to place organically as time permitted. For now, he felt a sense of pride and responsibility to do his part for the very freedom he was blessed with.

CHAPTER

3

"Boot Camp"

The morning had finally come for Jacob to head off to boot camp, and after a futile attempt by Ms. Goodchild to sway him from following through, it was apparent he had made up his mind once and for all. Ms. Goodchild's intentions were honorable, even though she fully believed in the cause to defend the United States and their involvement in WW2. She knew Jacob was entering as a 17 year old, which was the problem she had with it all. Breaking the rules wasn't something that she took lightly, and she made a final plea to Jacob to at least reconsider until his birthday later that year. It was wartime after all, and this was serious business as the call of duty seemed to beckon young men across each town throughout the land. Ms. Goodchild had a soft spot for Jacob and was certainly worried for his safety, but after he explained his burning desire to fight for his country and do the right thing, she knew he had his mind made up, and she retreated from her petition, while fully respecting his decision.

He was excited, nervous and hid his secret fears; his mom and dad were heavy on his mind this morning as he wanted to make them proud, but at the same time, the fear of death was still fresh in his mind. With his future still unknown, there were many things he had yet to experience, like his first love, traveling outside his small town, the great bond of friendship besides his own family members, and much more. Jacob had a way of compartmentalizing these thoughts and safely tucking the fears away shortly after they entered his mind. He justified his decisions, usually by knowing the truths behind them and realizing the foundation of good that upheld their righteousness.

The walk to the local bus station was less than a mile, and Jacob and Ms. Goodchild kept the conversation light along the way. Jacob would be heading to the Great Lakes Naval Training Center about 40 miles north of Chicago, and it would be a two-hour bus ride from his hometown. Knowing there was no turning back now, as the reality was setting in for both Jacob and Ms. Goodchild. So much had happened in the past several months; it was like a whirlwind for the entire Steele family. In some ways each member was forced to move on with their lives swifter than usually expected of children their age, as if time was unfairly stolen from their youth. In his wildest dreams, Jacob couldn't have imagined losing both of his parents, almost losing their home, the discovery of oil on their property, his country being at war, and now joining the fight. Life had certainly hit the Steele family like a ton of bricks and for better or worse, they all had grown up faster than planned.

The goodbye was brief, as Ms. Goodchild prayed with Jacob one last time before he got on his bus. "Be safe, and take care of yourself, young man," she offered as her final farewell. To which Jacob responded, "Always!" As he made his way to his designated seat, Jacob noticed the young faces of some of the passengers. They were filled with uncertainty and apprehension. He placed his knapsack on his seat, and taking his place near the middle of the bus, he scooted toward the window. There she was, just as she had always been, waving with a forced smile on her face. Jacob waved and nodded his head as if to say, "I know, I know." An officer entered the bus and welcomed the young men, reminding them how proud their country was that they joined the fight against tyranny. Within 20 minutes, they shoved off and headed toward their destination.

There was a quiet, somber feeling amongst the young men and the sounds of the bus engine and tires moving swiftly among the rough road were all that could be heard. A young man interrupted the silence, introducing himself to Jacob, "Hi, I'm Henry, my friends call me Hank." Shaking his hand, Jacob replied, "I'm Jacob Steele, good to meet you, Hank." The two-hour drive seemed to go faster as they approached the place they'd call "boot camp" for the next several weeks before they would be shipped abroad. Knowing that each man would soon be expected to be ready for battle at a moment's notice, a palpable fear that pervaded the base, mostly for the unexpected, as this was the first time most of these boys had been away from home. The tears in their mom's eyes flashed within each of their minds, as they also recalled the final lectures from their proud fathers. Some were joining out of necessity; unsure about the next chapters of their lives, the military offered that "in between" time to figure things out. For others, the military offered stability, and for some, it was the call of duty that persuaded them. While they were from all walks of life, here was an unspoken sense of equality among the young men. Neither race nor religion, or even background mattered in this scenario. They were well aware that the young man sitting next to them might just be the one who saves their life, and vice versa, a thought that didn't escape Jacob.

Hank and Jacob chatted throughout the drive and realized they had some things in common, like coming from a large family. Hank had four brothers and two sisters, and he was also the "baby" of the family. He lived in a rural area and spent much of his time enjoying life in the countryside. Like Jacob, he had a modest background, and had also experienced loss as his eldest brother died of cancer. Jacob opened up a little about losing his parents and the subsequent feelings of loss in his life. Realizing he was opening up more than usual, he knew it was sometimes easier to talk to strangers about personal things than to expose his vulnerabilities to people closest to him. Both young men felt a little more comfortable having someone to talk to as they were entering into uncharted territories.

Before long, the Naval Training Center was in their sights, and there was a sense of awe amongst the young men at the size of the facility from afar, and gazed at the sprawling fields that lay behind a giant gated area that protected the many buildings strewn about. There was a hustle and bustle of jeeps and cadets marching in unison in a very orderly and organized fashion. As the bus entered the facility, the hearts of the young men beat a little faster as life as they'd known it was about to change forever. When the bus came to a stop, the commanding officer stood and announced, "Here we are, men this will be your home for the next few weeks. Stay focused, stay diligent, and follow orders! We'll exit the bus starting from the front to back; please grab your bags and meet by that flagpole (as he pointed to its direction) in rows of four."

The men exited the bus and took their place as directed. Once they were in order, a distinguished gentleman in a decorated uniform approached them. "Welcome men, I'm Sergeant Moore, and for the next several weeks, you will train hard and learn your duties as Navy men who will be fully prepared to engage in battle if necessary! The man standing next to you is now your brother and we will work together as a team at all times. We are only as strong as each link of a chain, and there will be much expected of you, as you become the very best you can be! We will call your names, followed by your bunk building, and you will immediately go there and unpack. An officer will join shortly to give you your next orders. Again, welcome to the Navy. Your country is proud of you!"

Assignments were given, and Jacob was assigned to building F. He grabbed his knapsack and headed to the building with a large "F" painted in white. After finding his bunk, he unloaded his few belongings in the small dresser by the bed. He wasn't sure what to do next as he casually acknowledged each entering soldier with a head nod. He felt a hand slightly grab his shoulder and was happy to see it was Hank. "Hey, buddy, we're in the same group." Jacob grinned "That's great. It's good to see a familiar face in here." There was a palpable sense of apprehension among the young men as they scurried to find their places in the facility. There was uncertainty as each man was in an unfamiliar place with unfamiliar faces, waiting to be told what to do next.

Shortly thereafter, an officer and his assistant entered the building. "I'm Officer Simms," he announced. "I'll be in charge of you gentlemen during training. This is Officer Andrews, who will be calling out your names individually and handing you a ticket to pick up your uniforms in building B. Please listen carefully and exit in an orderly and efficient fashion. Once you pick up your uniforms, please return to your bunks from the back entrance and get dressed and wait for your next orders." Officer Simms began calling names as each soldier headed off one by one to pick up their uniforms.

The next hour passed, bringing with it a sense of comfort as Jacob accepted that this was the next chapter of his life. Some of the fear had faded, and he inhaled slowly, knowing that he was where he was supposed to be. A natural hard worker, Jacob felt confident that he would become the best soldier he could be, all while diligently focusing on his duties and training. He held his head high as he looked proudly at himself in uniform. There was a noticeable change in the young farm boy that came with life experience, as some of the hard times had weathered and even fortified a once innocent and naïve young boy to a strong and mature gentleman. Jacob paid attention to these small details and wanted to be the best at whatever he was doing. As he tied his boots, there was a sense of relief as the image of his mother and father came to his mind, and warmth filled his heart.

CHAPTER

4

"Preparing for War"

Mornings were early, afternoons were long, and evenings were short during training. Jacob had little time to reflect upon everything that had happened over the last several months. Moments were few and far between for any in-depth conversations amongst the trainees because they were busy jogging, marching, field training, organizing, learning, and just plain too exhausted. However, Jacob and Hank spent the little time they had getting to know each better, and had bonded nicely as friends. Christopher had joined their small crew of buddies, too, and offered the comic relief needed during the intense boot camp. He was from Arkansas and had a great sense of humor, as well as a drawl that helped in his delivery of some funny and timely stories. Most of the conversation between them took place in the "mess hall" or during the few breaks they were afforded, or sometimes at night before "lights out."

"Maybe I'm having these deep dreams from the exhaustion," Jacob thought to himself as he tried to comprehend the newest of his night visions. A fire had been stoked within him from his self-conscious that had him reminiscing. A bit of homesickness was possibly another reason he was envisioning his once happy and peaceful family life back on the farm. Only a few years removed from those days, it now seemed like a lifetime ago for Jacob. Mama and Papa would never again dance in the living room, laugh on the porch, or have conversations at the dinner table with all of their kids. There would be no more prayer groups with the family led by Ms. Goodchild, nor the hustle and bustle at breakfast before school. So much had changed, and although life had gone on for the Steele children in their own right, the trauma that led to the demise of his parents particularly stayed with Jacob in the form of a deep-recessed melancholy.

The previous night's dream had the entire Steele Family inside the town's church. Many of the locals were there, too, as they watched Mama and Papa walk down the aisle. It was a wedding-like scene, but everybody was older versions of themselves. Ms. Goodchild was at the altar with her Bible in hand, while all the Steele siblings stood on each side of her. The school choir was singing hymns, and everybody was happy and celebrating in the convivial setting. The pangs of rain were pelting the tiny church hard when suddenly a flush of water broke through the roof and begin filling up the church. It was all in slow motion as Jacob found himself swimming to help his family. For some reason, everybody appeared to be at peace except him. The ceremony seemed to be going on, and the only one concerned about what was happening seemed to be Jacob. While the details were vivid, he couldn't remember anything more about the dream.

There was little time for him to focus on the details of his subconscious thoughts, and he hesitated to share them with Hank or Christopher, so he kept it to himself. It was time to eat, and Jacob always looked forward to his moments his moments in the mess hall with his friends. It seemed like the trainees were always hungry, which wasn't surprising since they had been pushed to their physical and psychological limits during boot camp. Jacob met up first with Christopher and they grabbed their tray of food and sat down. Hank joined them shortly thereafter and immediately inhaled his glass of milk and wiped his mouth. "I just heard we're shipping off next Thursday and headed to Europe, not sure exactly where, but it is happening, boys!"

The other two paused eating and processed what Hank had just said. "Man, I hope we all stay together," offered Christopher. "Yeah, that would be great," Jacob agreed as he shoveled another spoonful of potatoes into his mouth, while trying to hide his feeling of concern. The three continued chatting but mostly about things other than war, and before long they were laughing about one thing or another, as usual.

Officers Simms and Andrews were talking privately at one end of the mess hall, and it looked serious. Jacob, aware of this, slowly focused his peripheral on them, while trying not to make it too obvious. Christopher and Hank were unaware of this, as Christopher continued a story about a time when he and his brother were fishing. He had just caught a fish and was bragging to his brother how skilled of a fisherman he was, when all of a sudden their dog Buster jumped up and grabbed the fish off his line and went running off. Chris's brother William couldn't stop laughing. Hank tried his best not to "crack up" too loudly, and although Jacob was eyeing the officers, he heard the jest of the story enough to appreciate it and laugh, too. Christopher had a way of lightening up the mood, and they all needed a little of that at the moment.

Before bed that night, they were finally allowed to listen to President Roosevelt's "Fireside Chats." It was February 23rd, 1942, and President Roosevelt's voice sounded strong and stoic as he spoke on the "Progress of the War." The men sat in silence as they hung on every word relayed from the old radio. It was certainly a reminder of why they were there and a timely morale booster to listen to the strong and unmistakable voice of Franklin Delano Roosevelt who asserted himself with character and leadership.

There was an unspoken understanding as the young men went to bed that night—a feeling of much needed support and unity. President Roosevelt's voice and powerful message somehow brought with it a level of comfort. Where there once was a recent air of confusion and concern, there was now a replaced sense of connection and definitiveness of purpose amongst the trainees. A couple of the quiet cadets had now assimilated nicely with the others, and some of the more boisterous men had humbly mellowed into leaders by example. Jacob, a cerebral gentlemen by nature, took it all in. He visualized a chain—where the stronger links would withstand the heavier loads when the weaker ones couldn't, while knowing that this process would alternate as needed. The men were a team, and although they would likely be split up as they went to war, the lessons of working together had been indelibly embedded in them.

Jacob had a renewed sense of clarity that night and decided it was a good time to write a letter to his family. Since everybody was geographically spread out, it made the most sense to write to Miss Goodchild and have her relay his message to the rest. He also wanted to ease Ms. Goodchild's mind as he knew she was concerned about him being away from home for the first time, especially with all that he personally had endured these last several months.

Dear Ms. Goodchild & my dear brothers and sisters,

I'm writing you on this evening of February 23rd, 1942 from boot camp. The last couple of weeks have brought with them a lot of hard training, both physical and mental. I am stronger because of it and thankful I am part of a great crew, with whom I've made several friends. That being said, I have experienced a bit of homesickness because I miss you all dearly. Knowing I am part of something positive with regard to the fight for our country helps to get me through those longings for home and family. I also know we are deeply connected on a level that transcends time and space, and I hold that dearly in my heart. I had a dream about Mama and Papa the other night, and you all were in it. Although it was confusing at times (like dreams can be), we were all together in celebration and this brought a smile to my face. I can't wait to tell you more about that and all the things I will be experiencing when I see you all again, and I anxiously await to hear all the stories of your adventures, too. I hope that is sooner rather than later! I miss every single one of you and look forward to the day we can be together again. I'll be shipping off soon, and I will correspond as able.

Lovingly,

Jacob

Jacob folded the letter in thirds, placed it in the envelope, and addressed it. He would put it in the mail drop the following day. Expressing himself to his family made him feel good, and even though he felt a tear welling up in the corner of his eye, the thought of each of his siblings, Mama, Papa, and Ms. Goodchild brought a visual recall of each of them, like snapshots in his mind. Jacob possessed an ability to remember moments in his life clearly, along with a visual connection of that moment. This usually served him well, especially in times of sentimental reflection. However, in moments where he experienced trauma, like the death of each of his parents, it played a role of disservice to his mental state. He didn't mention the other details of his dream in the letter about the water filling the church, and his frantic attempt to save everyone, as he was still privately processing it himself. Nonetheless, tonight, Jacob went to bed feeling strong, proud, and grateful. He would experience his best night's sleep since the beginning of boot camp and had a serene dream of the sun glistening on him as he floated peacefully in the ocean.

CHAPTER

5

"The Letter"

Recognizing Jacob's handwriting, her hands trembled as she looked at the envelope. It had been over two months since she said goodbye to him at the bus station. It served as a bittersweet moment for her as she was proud of the boy who was turning into a man with a strong sense of values and duty, but she would also miss that young boy who had needed her so much, and became like a son to her. She had a soft spot for Jacob as he had seen so much at such a young age. He carried the pain from the loss of his parents, especially the manner in which he found his father that fateful day deep inside the recesses of his soul, and Ms. Hannah Goodchild wanted nothing more than to help him heal. However, he was likely an ocean away fighting for his country, while the once tight knit Steele family was spread out by time and space.

She slid her fingers along the top of the envelope and carefully ripped it the open, revealing the letter inside. She took a deep breath; knowing Jacob finally had sent correspondence eased her mind momentarily, but an anxiousness also pervaded her thoughts. She was a faithful and God-fearing woman whose beliefs ran deep, but the fear of the unknown can be a very unsettling thing. Fear of loss can be downright scary. There was a vulnerability within the Steele family after having experienced not only the painful losses of both Mama and Papa, but also the manner in which their demise unfolded. It was an unspoken thought, but every one of them knew that the stresses of life took such a toll that it made them susceptible to illnesses.

A sudden sense of relief eased Ms. Goodchild's heart as she read the words, "Dear Ms. Goodchild & my dear brothers and sisters." Her breathing slowed as the tear that had lingered on the edge of her eye finally dropped onto the letter, representing both fear and joy. Hoping that Jacob was still in good spirits now, as he seemed to be when he wrote this letter, Ms. Goodchild said a silent prayer for the boy she had helped raise and whom she considered a son. There was a sense of inherited maternal responsibility she felt for the entire Steele family, and she wanted nothing but the best for all of them, while reveling in the thought that they would all be back together under the same roof someday soon.

Although Hannah Goodchild-Steele was the second wife and widow of Abraham Steele, the children always referred to her as Ms. Goodchild, and this was fine by her because she knew it was not only out of habit, but also a symbol of respect from her role as a teacher, mentor, confidant, and friend. She preferred this too, as she never wanted them to feel as though she was trying to replace their beloved mother. She accepted the role as surrogate mom because of her love for the family and the promise she made to Sara Steele. She also accepted the role as Abraham Steele's wife and caretaker; at the time, she was spending most of the time caring for the entire family after teaching all day, and being a woman of faith, she wouldn't move in unless she was properly married. This was the one contradiction she battled inside, as her feelings for Abraham weren't rooted in affection, passion, or true love. She believed God would approve of the arrangement because her heart was pure in wanting to be there for the entire family, whom she loved deeply as a whole.

She came into the family when it was in disarray following the death of Sara Steele. It was a tall task for anyone, but her commitment to them transcended everything. Papa's drinking had gotten out of control, and bills were piling up. Still, she took on the task as mother, housekeeper, farmhand, cook, bookkeeper, and counselor. She knew the liability she faced financially, too, as the wife of Abraham Steele at that time; it was a lot of stress, debt, and hard work. However, she carried on, prayed on, and never wavered in her faith. With all the difficulties they endured, blessings came soon thereafter. Although the void from the losses of Mama and Papa could never be filled, the Steele children were all thriving in their own right.

Soon after oil was discovered on the Steele property, Ms. Goodchild started a trust in each of the kids' names and they were allotted a monthly income for the rest of their lives that provided much needed security. She knew that money could change people, and didn't want them to have a windfall of money after having endured poverty, as it could have spun them into an overindulgent lifestyle. The farmhouse was paid off, and she spent her mornings tending to the crops, animals, and home prior to heading to the schoolhouse to teach and influence Stoney Point's youth. On Saturdays, she could be found selling produce, quilts, and preserves at the farmers' market and used most of the proceeds to buy supplies for the school and donate to the church. On Sunday mornings, she attended church and then returned home for some cooking, sewing, and reading. She lived a simple, but happy, life and was considered by everyone to be a strong, faithful, and independent woman who was committed to God and family.

So much had happened over the last year. Two of the boys Gary, and Jacob now fighting in the war, while Mark and Keith, who were already young veterans themselves, were partners in a farm supply company in Iowa. Luis and Lane were making names for themselves in the midwest boxing circuit as they worked toward big ticket fights. The Steele sisters Jenny, Scarlet, and Lauren, and Susie had all married and moved away, but stayed in touch mostly through letters, which Ms. Goodchild kept tucked away in a safe place. She would often read them while sitting on her favorite sewing chair by the fire. Seven of the Steele children had returned home briefly to attend the funeral of their beloved friend and midwife, Mrs. McDougal, who had passed away last fall. Bessie Ann was now married and still lived in Stoney Point, where she cleaned houses and was a part-time nanny for some of the wealthy residents. Once a month, she would help Ms. Goodchild sell her goods at the farmers market, and they became very good friends.

She counted the many blessings she had and never focused on what her life might have been had she accepted proposals from her pursuers many years ago. She knew romance and courtship were fleeting, and her deep connections to her inherited family and God were rooted in goodness. Her commitment was stronger than ever to keep the family tightly knitted together, while maintaining the good name of Abraham and Sara Steele, as well as their children.

She opened the old tin bread box and added Jacob's letter to the many others from her stepchildren. She closed her eyes, clasped her hands, and slowly dropped to her knees and began praying:

"Heavenly Father, please keep them all safe and sound. Protect them from harm's way, and give them comfort in time of need. Please fill their hearts with your love and the love from each other. Let them be reminded of the power of faith, family, and good deeds. Give them comfort in their hearts and minds. Forgive us all of our sins and shortcomings, Lord, and I ask you for strength to keep moving forward in my efforts to be a good example for our children. Please help us all to see the light and help to end this war, while bringing our boys home safely. I ask you to protect our family and home. I await the reunion of our boys and girls faithfully and will rejoice in your name, my dear Lord and Savior. Amen."

She then tucked away the bread box of letters on the top shelf of the pantry, wiped the tears from her eyes and lit a hearty fire. She began sewing and reminiscing about the past and all the school children who had hope and wonder in their eyes while she stood in front of the class. She knew teaching had found her, and blessed her with the opportunity to touch the lives of the innocent, and play a role in their education of life. It was more than just arithmetic, spelling, writing, and reading. Children look up to adults as role models to help guide the way. Their hearts and minds are open canvasses, and Ms. Hannah Goodchild had known from a very young age, that she could touch the world and make a difference one child at a time through teaching. This brought her great fulfillment. It was through her love and compassionate heart that each member of the Steele family, especially Jacob, felt safer and happier.

CHAPTER

6

"The Battle Begins"

Excitement, pride, and fear of the unknown were at the forefront of Jacob's mind as he boarded the first ship he'd ever been on. This was a far cry from life on a farm for a country boy used to a modest rural setting. His eyes widened as he shook hands with the commanding officer and received his orders and bunk assignment. He had always dreamt bigger than the town in which he grew up, and knew that the butterflies in his stomach were all part of his growth; a reminder that getting out of his comfort zone meant he was about to fulfill his dream of seeing the great big world he'd only read about in books and magazines. Jacob had endured a lot in the last year and was fortified by tough times, but he still carried with him a hidden vulnerability. He was prepared and excited to fight for the country he loved, yet certainly wasn't disillusioned by the idea that this tour of duty would come without danger. In some ways, he felt he needed to redeem himself and his family name. Two of his brothers were serving, and Jacob was very proud of them, yet he needed this adventure and experience to fill the void from the loss of his parents.

It was a busy morning as hundreds of young men navigated through the process of being in their correct and respective units. There was a palpable sense of excitement and confusion, and although boot camp had prepared them for many things, this seemed larger than life. For most of them, it was an entirely different world from what they knew or expected. It was wartime, and that fact hit differently than being a sailor during times of peace. The Navy seemed to be made up of two types of recruits: those who were there because of a family tradition, and those who were escaping something, and this time away from their home would give them perspective and direction. Jacob, too was searching for purpose and adventure.

Eventually, things settled into a semblance of order while several men worked their way into the berths to unpack their belongings and meet their bunk mates. Jacob was organizing his modest belongings as a baby-faced sailor entered. "Hello, I'm Jacob Steele," greeted Jacob. "Howdy, I'm Victor Noel," the soldier replied as the two extended their arms for a firm handshake. "Welcome, Victor, feel free to choose your spot as I'm good with either bed." "Why thank you, it doesn't matter to me either," Victor responded in his southern drawl. "Okay," Jacob patted the bed nearest him, "I'll take this one here. "I'm from Shelby, Tennessee. What about you?" "I'm from a small town called Stoney Point, Illinois," replied Jacob. Victor nodded, and they both went about their business of getting settled in as they made small talk.

Jacob pulled out his diary and placed it under his thin mattress, anxious to make some new entries later that day as time and privacy permitted. There was so much he wanted to write about, especially his anticipation to be at sea and their eventual destination in Europe. He knew Miss Goodchild would be worried about him and any correspondence would not only be welcomed by her, but also shared with his siblings. The thought of her reading his letters gave Jacob momentary comfort as he pictured the relief on the faces of his family, who would most certainly be concerned about his well-being.

Both Jacob and Victor confirmed that their orders were to meet on deck in one hour for orientation. There certainly wasn't any tolerance for tardiness on the ship, especially on their first day which the commanding officer made very clear. They finished organizing their belongings and decided to walk up early to meet up with the rest of the new crew. Jacob knew Hank and Christopher were somewhere on board. While he hadn't seen them yet, he certainly looked forward to it. He grinned as he thought of the nickname their boot camp officer gave the trio: "The Three Musketeers."

Victor was in awe of the large vessel that he and the men would call home for the next several months. "Would you look at this? It's like a floating city," he remarked. Jacob nodded in agreement as they reached the upper deck, and the light offered a landscape view of the ship against the open waters. Neither was sure exactly where they would end up in Europe, as they weren't privy to such information yet, but they'd heard whispers that the transatlantic crossing would take up to three weeks. During this time, the Navy's primary role in Europe was to support the Army's operations while providing transport for troops and supplies, as well as gunfire, if needed. Uncertainties were prevalent at this stage, as the war was gaining momentum and the U.S. involvement intensified.

Awaiting their directions, the two of them joined up with several of the other men. Roll call began several minutes later, and lines were formed as officers, donned in their full Naval regalia, organized the divisions based on assignments. Indoctrinations followed, and each sailor would soon learn the basics of their respective jobs. Jacob and Victor began to understand the concept behind "running a tight ship" as things slowly became clearer. Jacob spotted Hank from afar, but didn't dare attempt to call out to him while the officers spoke. There would be plenty of time to catch up later, and he knew he had to focus on the overview of the ship's operations and safety procedures being discussed.

Day one would prove to be a long and exhausting day, after which the food awaiting them at mess hall was welcomed by all. Like everything else on board, there was an orderly process for eating times, as well. As luck would have it, the mess hall would be the exact place where "The Three Musketeers" would reunite. Their familiar faces were a sight for sore eyes, as Hank, Christopher, and Jacob found a spot to chow down and catch up. After some casual greetings were exchanged, the trio discussed the day's events and shared their perspectives on day one, and what the future might hold for them on the ship, as well as in the war.

France had become occupied by the Nazis, and Hitler's evil was wreaking havoc on that part of the world. President Roosevelt knew there was no choice but to go full force against tyranny as freedom was being threatened worldwide. War had been declared not only by Japan with their attack on Pearl Harbor, but Germany, too, was looming over the United States with their declaration of war. It seemed implausible that one dictator was capable of so much terror, which had now become a worldwide problem.

The boys sat at their table and shared their opinions on what to expect but none of them had any idea what was lurking in Europe. They did, however, have the gumption to lay their lives on the line, if needed, in order to protect the very freedoms they'd been afforded. "I haven't seen my brothers in almost a year," chimed Jacob. They're risking their lives for our country, and we've got to do our part." "I'd love nothing more than to stare that evil son of a gun down one on one; just give me five minutes with that sick tyrant!" exclaimed Hank. "We've got to stick together, boys. No matter what happens, we've got to stick together!" said Christopher. It was the most serious they'd ever seen him, and when he placed his hand on the table, Jacob and Hank immediately responded by placing their hands on top of his. "We promise," they simultaneously and solemnly vowed.

The mood lightened quickly as the conversation turned into their typical lighthearted chit chat. Before long they headed to their respective bunks and called it a night. Jacob entered his room and noticed that Victor was on his knees finishing up his prayers. To avoid startling him, he respectfully slowed his movement and Victor rose to his feet and greeted Jacob, "Hey, Jacob, I was just saying my prayers, kind of an old habit of mine from back home." "Good to know I have a faithful roommate. We could all use some prayers, for sure, I do praying each day, too," confessed Jacob. He wanted Victor to feel comfortable, and this scenario allowed Jacob to open up a bit as he went on to explain how Miss Goodchild was a God-fearing woman and kept the tradition of prayer in their home. Although both young men were exhausted, they spent the next hour opening up about their lives.

CHARACTER

7

"Torpedoed"

The ship was cutting through the English Channel cautiously as the captain reiterated that Germans had been known to target vessels in this area. Within moments, tension pervaded the crew, as radar had reported enemy submarines in the area. A red alert had been given as the alarms sounded and within seconds there was the explosion. They were hit! A disabling torpedo blow had decimated the once strong and stoic ship. Jacob's ears were ringing as confusion and shock filled his head. He knew he had to snap out of it and put his thoughts into action as he muddled his way through the murky waters filled with oil, fire, and debris. "This is really happening," he muttered to himself, then took a long inhaled breath and assessed his surroundings.

Their ship had been attacked and blown to pieces, and his instincts kicked in as he swam from body to body, trying to keep crewmembers afloat. One by one, he lifted heads from the water only to find that most of them had perished in the blast. Two other members moaned from a distance as he swam fiercely toward them. He could barely recognize

Christopher, whose face was bloodied and covered with oil. Jacob, with his arm badly burned himself, pulled Christopher up and tried to ignore the exposed skin and blood that seemed to glisten from the oily waters. He then made his way to a captain he recognized as "Flaherty." The scarce moans fell eerily upon his slightly muted ears that had been temporarily deafened from the explosions. Almost everyone was dead! Tears burned from his eyes as the salt water from the ocean ominously paired with the salt of his tears, as he was overcome with helplessness. "Where's Hank?" he sobbed as he stabilized the two men upon the floating mangled debris. Jacob made sure they were aware enough to hold on while he frantically searched for Hank.

What seemed like hours, was more like minutes, but the moment he came upon the very first friend he ever made on that bus heading to Boot Camp that fateful day, he would never forget, as he looked at the face on his lifeless buddy Hank. It would be a reminder of the senseless cruelty of war, and a constant questioning of the nature of the very species in which he belonged. "Why?" he screamed with the seemingly last few pockets of air that remained in his lungs. Hank's kind nature and hospitable personality was what helped Jacob survive boot camp, and now the legacy of his fallen friend would be the driving force and fire that would burn deep inside him for the rest of his living days. "Not on my watch!" he moaned as he vowed then and there that Hank's life and death would not be in vain.

The three of them stayed afloat by hanging on to a 4 x 3 piece of the ship, while Jacob shifted back and forth to maintain buoyancy for them. It had been two to three hours since the attack, and there was no help in sight. Drowning was his first fear, being captured by the enemy, next, followed closely by sharks, then dehydration. "Any one of these would be a terrible way to die," he thought. He reached over to Flaherty and slightly slapped him back to consciousness as he was fading from exhaustion. He alternated between the captain and Christopher, making sure they didn't slip off their float or fall asleep. He originally thought they could take turns resting while the two stayed awake, but it was too dangerous, as none of them would be able to sleep while holding on, so they rested their eyes one by one, as Jacob made sure to arouse them back into alertness with a slap and/or tug of what was left of their sleeves.

As Jacob's mind drifted, irony slowly seeped into his consciousness; here he was clinging to dear life in a body of water filled with oil from the ship as he sharply looked death in the eyes. An unintentional grin and grunt came to him, as it was oil that ultimately saved his family's home after his Papa had passed, and now he might die in the very substance that once was his savior. In Jacob's first business savvy act, he recalled going to the bank and asking them for a 30 day extension on the foreclosure of their house and farm, which they immediately denied. He went to the library and researched extensively about the legal time frames in the state of Illinois with regard to nonpayment foreclosure and found that by law they had 60 days from the time of the notice of foreclosure to pay the arrears on the mortgage, and thirty days to communicate their intentions, which he did, and another thirty days to get caught up before their home could be taken from them.

On a quest to keep their family home, Jacob spent the next several days researching the plot of land where their family lived and spoke to neighbors, a judge, college professors, and anybody who might be able to help him with information. He was intrigued as to why the bank was in such a hurry to repossess their property and get them out of there through means that seemed questionable. He was able to talk to a friend of an old neighbor who explained to Jacob that the bank had given them a substantial sum of money for their home several months before when they hadn't even been in the market to sell. Jacob's instincts turned out to be right, as he knew their property was worth much more than the edifices above ground.

It wasn't the house, the barn, the farm or the land that the bank was interested in, as much as what was under the ground of their property: oil! In the nick of time Jacob negotiated a deal whereby he would allow a small parcel of land to be used for oil production, while keeping the family home and farm. The Steele's were paid a handsome sum of money for this, and each of them profited comfortably, including Ms. Goodchild, who was there helping and guiding Jacob along the way. She was hesitant to accept any money, until Jacob reminded her she could use the funds for the local school house, thus benefitting many young students for years to come. This spoke to her soul and she put the money to good use for the benefit of others.

Oil had saved their home, and although it came a bit late after Papa's death, it provided the stability the Steele family needed desperately after so much despair. Mama and Papa would have been so proud of Jacob for stepping up in their time of need and helping his siblings. Jacob remembered Ms. Goodchild gathering all the children and praising God for His miraculous ways.

That was the last time they had all been together, and the memory had stoked so many emotions for Jacob that it immediately snapped him back into his current ordeal; He took action by making sure his two crew members were still alive. Several hours had now passed, and young Flaherty was fading. He was mumbling inaudibly as he had ingested so much salt water and oil that it was causing him to dry heave what was left in his system. Dehydration had set in, and he gasped for air. The look in his eyes was that of defeat as he slowly released his grip and submerged himself. Jacob dove and retrieved him, trying his best to lift him up. "Chris, help, help!" Jacob cried, as they both did their best to hang on to their flotation device with one hand, and Flaherty with another. They struggled for the next several minutes to reattach his hands to the float but he had faded into unconsciousness. They both checked him over several times to see if he was still breathing. Unfortunately, he was gone! Although their efforts were commendable, it served no consolation, and the tormenting decision to release him to the depths of the ocean had to be made, as they both wept.

Although they were surrounded by the vastness of the ocean water, it served no immediate purpose for what they needed most: fresh water! Jacob and Chris were dehydrated, and they needed drinkable water desperately. It had been two days since Flaherty had been gone, and the sun was beating down on the two sole survivors. They had drunk small amounts of sea water just to keep their throat and lips from drying up, but this provided no relief for their thirst. In fact, the salt in the water only increased their need for fresh water. "Ironic," Jacob thought once again, how there was more water around them than he'd ever seen in his life, and none of it could help quench his thirst. He realized he might die while surrounded by the very substance that he needed to stay alive.

A few times during their ordeal, Jacob had fallen asleep only to be awakened underneath the water as he struggled to get back to surface. This time he briefly thought of surrendering himself to the sea, as his will to live was dwindling; "Why has death surrounded me?" he thought. As he reflected upon Mama and Papa's passing, now Hank was gone and the trauma from this devastation had weakened his instinct to survive. During these moments, he wanted out of this world, he wanted the pain and sadness to end, and he thought for a brief moment about giving up. It had crossed his mind of just letting go, and even attempted to drown himself but instincts took over and after he had an out-of-body experience of being lifted up by an outstretched arm, he couldn't go through with it. He couldn't recognize who or what was bringing him up, but he knew he wasn't alone out there. He wanted to die, but a force far greater wouldn't concede, as if to say, "It's not your time, you have a purpose in this life, now live it!"

On the third time down, a moment of clarity came to Jacob as he pondered the idea of converting salt water to fresh water, thus providing the very substance that could save him. "Why am I still alive?" he thought, and at that moment his wake-up call aroused him and ignited his will to live, to save Christopher, and to spend the rest of his days on this Earth with a purpose of helping others. It would be several more hours until a rescue boat came to them and pulled them from the ocean. They sopped up all the fresh water on board that they were given, and slowly but surely, the life-giving liquid pulsed through their veins and brought them back to full awareness. This awareness came with the somber fact that everybody else had died which brought humility and sadness to the two survivors.

It would be almost a full day before Jacob woke up in a makeshift hospital room run by the Red Cross. He was disoriented as he looked around and slowly realized where he was. He saw row upon row of injured soldiers in the dark, dank room, and he mustered up all his energy to call out for someone. Within a few moments, a nurse came to him and said, "Sir, take it easy, you must not exert yourself." "Christopher, Christopher, where is Christopher?" Jacob cried out. "He's asleep a few beds over," as she pointed to his whereabouts. "Is he going to be alright?" Jacob asked. "Yes, he's resting now. You've both been through a lot and are lucky to be alive. Now it is imperative that you rest and heal, and soon you'll be able to go home." Jacob looked into her blue eyes, and they reminded him of the ocean where he almost died. But instead of the vast, unpredictable waters he had recently faced, her ocean blue eyes brought him a sense of hope. Her voice brought him calmness. Her presence brought him back to life! Maggie was her name, and right then and there, under the most precarious of settings, Jacob had secretly and privately vowed to marry her one day!

CHAPTER

8

"The Hospital"

He could hear the back and forth creaking of wood coming from the next room. Jacob slowly approached the doorway and upon entering, his heart dropped, as he tried to interpret what he was looking at. Then it all hit him in an instant. It was Papa hanging from a rope, just as he last saw him that fateful day, years ago. The scene unfolded in slow motion as Jacob ran toward him methodically, although his legs were moving sluggishly as if underwater. He was trying desperately to reach him in time to cut the rope, or at least, lift him up before he gasped his last breath. Jacob's movements slowed even more, as he attempted to move forward, almost as if he was fighting an invisible but resistant force. But when he finally got to him, it was too late. A split second thereafter, they were rocked by an explosion, and their farm was under attack by enemy torpedoes, followed by loud and repetitive gunfire. Everything in the room was being decimated by bullets, then small fires broke out. While he knew it was too late to save his father, Jacob rushed to cut Papa down before bullets riddled his lifeless body.

He scurried to find a knife, but as he approached every option, the gunfire became dangerously close, preventing him from apprehending any sharp object that could cut the rope. His helplessness finally came to a crescendo with a blood-curdling scream.

"Jacob, Jacob, you're having a nightmare!" Maggie's soothing voice penetrated his ears as he opened his eyes. Catching his breath, he looked around the room. Disoriented at first, he began to familiarize himself with his whereabouts. Maggie placed her hand on his shoulder as she reached for a glass of water and said, "Here, Jacob, drink this slowly." Embarrassed, he grabbed the glass and took a drink. Maggie's comfort helped to offset any awkwardness he might have felt, as she chatted casually about the nightmares she also has. "I have this recurring dream that begins with me at my childhood home in Michigan and I can't find our dog." Her wispy voice and accentuation danced beautifully off her lips as Jacob glanced at her intermittently, noticing each of her beautiful features. She continued, "I can hear his moans and groans coming from the woods behind our house, and I keep looking for him, until I finally come upon him. I call out Sam, are you okay? But it's not really him; he's got fangs and he's bloody, and just as I realize this, I wake up, usually in a cold sweat and trying to catch my breath. I've tried to figure out what it means, but I realize it's just a dream. Our subconscious mind is a wonderful and strange thing." She smiled and said, "Now, you rest, Jacob, and I'll see you later."

Jacob inhaled, and assessed the room as he smiled, realizing that Maggie had really helped him feel better. He'd never met anyone quite like her, and her natural beauty was invigorating to him, as well as a bit daunting. He knew the more he thought about her, the more he wanted to be with her. For a moment, he daydreamed about them walking hand in hand by the lake, having picnics under a tree in the spring, and falling in love. Jacob tried to fight the doubt that was setting in, as the reality of his situation crept up on him; here he was, a wounded soldier, unsure where he was headed next, in constant pain, sitting in a makeshift hospital, and feeling a little sorry for himself. "How could someone in my condition ever land someone like her?" He whispered to himself under his breath.

It didn't take long for Jacob to snap out of his doldrums, realizing that in the beds next to him were soldiers in much worse shape than he. Amputations, and life-threatening wounds brought much greater challenges to those men, and he caught himself from heading further down the path of self-pity. Miss Hannah Goodchild would not accept such "woe is me" behavior. "Pick yourself up and dust yourself off, young man," she would say. "Don't feel sorry for yourself. Put one foot in front of the other and keep moving." He grinned as he imagined her saying this to him. He missed her and his siblings, dearly.

Christopher had been released earlier that week which was both good and sad news for Jacob, as he was the last person who felt like family to him. With homesickness setting in, Jacob focused on a design he'd been working on daily for a filtration system that could take sea water and filter out the salt so it would become drinkable water. This kept him occupied most of the day, and his notes were organized meticulously. Maggie and the other staff nurses had been very generous to him by providing paper, pencils, and a clipboard for his work. They would often ask about the project he was working on, and he would humbly answer, "Just a water purification system idea that popped into my head." It, of course, was much more detailed than that, as this idea, which came to him first in a dream, then in the moments he was submerged underwater after the attack by enemy torpedoes, was now his obsession.

As he continued outlining and labeling his renderings, he could hear all the noise around him as if he were back in the water searching for Hank. It was chaos and frightening to be part of war, as the worst in mankind reared its ugly head to the point of killing one another. At first, joining the war was a prideful act of valor and nationalism to him, but now after having witnessed death and destruction all around him, his views had been indelibly changed forever. Sure, he was proud to do his part as an American who knew there was evil lurking across the ocean and, unfortunately, the necessity to battle against such evil, but there was a part of him that realized the depth of war's casualties on man and mankind.

Jacob hadn't fully addressed the occurrence that took place underwater when he and the few others were clinging to life in the shark-infested, murky ocean. The fact that he felt the presence of God as he was ready to give up and sink to his death, seemed all too much for him to wrap his head around. However, as nightfall and quietness fell in the room, he was ready to deal with it. Initially, shame filled his mind, as he and God were the only two who knew the truth, who knew that he was ready to give up. Yes, exhaustion and pain were definitely part of the reason, but never in his life could he imagine giving in or giving up. This bothered him greatly, as he remembered his dad, a man he had so greatly admired as a young boy, had also given in to the bottle and gave up on life. This was somewhat of a reckoning for Jacob, as he realized man could be pushed to the brink of self-destruction. As he processed and battled his own demons, he felt forgiveness in his heart for his father.

He wanted to further understand why God had been with him underwater, and why he actually felt His hand pull him up. Was it just another one of his night visions that had entered his head during duress? It was, he thought, but all while he knew the answer was no! What Jacob experienced underwater was something he would never forget, nor would he ever stop trying to understand. He not only saw a light illuminate through oil-filled, dark waters, but it literally slowed the moment to a halt, while a force pulled him up like felines lifting up their cubs by the loose skin at the back of their neck. It was both gentle and powerful, and also an act of love. The thought brought tears to Jacob's eyes.

Placing his drawings in his knapsack at the side of his bed, he thought about that scenario for a moment. Miss Goodchild was the only person who he'd someday feel comfortable sharing this story with. But she was not here right now. She had faith so deep that it wouldn't seem like an awe-stricken moment to her, because she already possessed the belief that this could happen. Jacob didn't possess such deep faith, but he wanted to. He knew it would be a long road of recovery for him too, as he found himself at a crossroads in his young life. He would have to get back home and start his life over; he would have to figure out a way to reunite with Maggie; he would have to continue his work on a water filtration system that he truly believed could save lives; he would have to find a way to feel normal again after experiencing life-altering moments within the ugliness of war; and he would have to overcome his wounds, both physical and mental from a body and mind that had been forever changed.

CHAPTER

9

"The Homecoming"

Jacob's homecoming was not what anyone might call a triumphant return. There were no brass bands, no embraces on the train platform, no waiting arms of loved ones. Instead, there was silence—Missouri fields stretching flat and endless, a sky as wide as the ache in his chest, and the sense that he no longer belonged to this place, though it had once been home. Discharged and sent back with scars too deep for anyone to see at first glance. Jacob felt like a shadow of the boy who had left. He was placed back into civilian clothes, but the war had not loosened its grip.

He could not face the stares, the well-meaning neighbors who would say they were proud of him, or worse, ask him about the war. He could not walk up the porch steps of the family home that no longer existed as he remembered. Mama and Papa were gone. His siblings scattered, each with their own burdens. The idea of stepping into town felt like stepping onto a stage he wasn't prepared for. And so, instead of going home, Jacob rented a room in a worn-down motel on the outskirts of town. A bed, a lamp, a desk with a wobbling leg, and four pale walls— that became his world.

Nights were the hardest. His mind looped through memories of Hank, his friend who never came home, his laughter now silenced forever. He replayed the moments of chaos, the torpedoes, the oil-slick water, the screams. Some nights he could still smell the smoke and salt and blood. He lay awake until exhaustion finally stole him, only to drop him into dreams where Papa swung from a rope again and the war raged on without mercy.

The bar down the road became his refuge. Dim lights, stale air, the burn of whiskey down his throat, and the fog it blessed him with. At first it was just one drink to quiet the thoughts, then another to numb the pain in his body where the injuries still throbbed. The doctors had sent him off with morphine tablets for the worst of it, but Jacob found himself reaching for them more often than intended. Each pill a promise of silence, each drink an erasure of the man he feared he had become. The more he swallowed, the less he had to think about Hank, or Maggie, or the face of his father in that last terrible dream.

Yet, Maggie lingered in his mind. Her soft voice, her eyes that had seen his brokenness and hadn't flinched. He tucked her away, like a letter never sent, knowing he wasn't worthy of her kindness, not now. What could he offer her but a haunted man's hollow shell? He could not even bring himself to write her name on paper as if by doing so he would betray her by showing her what he had become.

Miss Goodchild's words came back to him in quiet moments, that old admonition to pick himself up, dust himself off, and keep moving forward. But instead of strength, her voice made him feel ashamed. He was not moving forward. He was sinking, the weight of survivor's guilt pressing him into the earth. Why had he been spared when better men had fallen? Hank should have been here, not him. Each swallow of whiskey seemed to answer *you don't deserve this life, but you're living it anyway.*

The memories of Mama and Papa surfaced often. He thought of Mama's warm hands, her singing voice on Sunday mornings, how she always had faith that God would carry them through. He thought of Papa, whose demons had driven him to the bottle and then to the rope. The image haunted Jacob most of all—not just because of the nightmare's cruelty, but because he felt himself edging closer to that same fate. He had sworn never to be like that guy his father eventually became. Now, alone in a motel room with empty bottles by the bed, he feared he was walking the same path.

Still, in the quiet hours when the liquor wore off and sleep refused him, Jacob pulled out his papers and pencils. He returned to the designs he had begun overseas; the dream of turning salt water into fresh, drinkable water. He sketched valves and filters, tanks and flowlines, erasing and redrawing with meticulous care. In these moments, he felt something stirring within, that was not despair. It was not exactly hope, but perhaps the whisper of purpose. The world was full of destruction, he knew that too well, but maybe—just maybe—he could build something that gave life instead of taking it.

Sometimes his hands trembled as he drew, not only from drinking but from the weight of everything pressing on him. Yet he pressed the pencil harder to the page, determined to bring form to the vision that had once come to him in the darkest water. God's hand, or madness, or both—he didn't know. But it was something to cling to, when everything else slipped away.

When dawn broke, he would often crumble his sketches into the wastebasket, ashamed of the small flicker of belief he had allowed himself. Other times he carefully folded them and placed them in his knapsack, as if saving them for a future he couldn't yet admit to. Jacob told himself he wasn't ready to see Miss Goodchild. She would look into his eyes and know too much. She would remind him of who he had been, who he could still be—and he wasn't sure he could bear that. Better to hide a while longer, to drown the guilt in another liquid, to let the world forget him as he tried to forget himself. But even as he numbed his body and mind, the drawings stacked slowly in his bag, each page a silent contradiction to the man he thought he was becoming. A drunk, a coward, a broken soldier. And yet—also, perhaps an inventor. A man still clinging to some shred of creation in the aftermath of so much destruction.

Jacob did not know it then, but those two selves—the man of despair and the man of design—were at war with him. And though he tried to smother it, the part of him that longed to build, to redeem, was not dead. If he could create something purposeful that saved lives instead of the man-made machines of war that destroyed them, maybe it could make him more deserving of the love he received from others. Maybe Hank would be proud of him for, and his death wouldn't be in vain. Maybe he would become the man he was supposed to be—the man Maggie saw through the lens of those piercing blue eyes. Maybe he could help his siblings better their lives, move closer and become the tight-knit family they all used to be. Maybe Mama and Papa somehow would know that their son had accomplished something great. Maybe Miss Goodchild wouldn't have to worry about him so much anymore, and all her prayers for him and his siblings would come to fruition. Maybe, he could overcome the pull of the pills and the bottle. Maybe!

CHAPTER

10

"Aimless"

One evening after drinking too much and stumbling into the cool night air, Jacob found himself walking without aim. The town slept, the wind whispering through empty streets, when the faint glow of a small church caught his eye. Its doors were open, candles flickering inside. Something in him, maybe desperation, maybe longing—drew him toward it. He stepped inside quietly, the scent of old wood and wax greeting him. The pews were empty save for one man kneeling in prayer at the front. Jacob sat in back, his hands trembling as he bowed his head. Ms. Goodchild's voice echoed softly in his memory: *"Prayer is a bridge between who you are and who you're meant to become. Even when you can't find the words, God hears the ache of your heart."*

He tried to pray, but the words caught in his throat. All he could manage was a whisper: "Why, Lord? Why me?" The sound of footsteps made him look up. A man in a dark vestment, an older pastor with kind eyes stood beside him. He didn't speak at first, just placed a steady hand on Jacob's shoulder and bowed his head in silent prayer. The gesture alone unraveled Jacob's defenses. For the first time in months, tears slipped freely down his face.

Later, they spoke quietly in the church office. The pastor listened more than he spoke, nodding as Jacob haltingly described the war, the loss of his friend Hank, the nightmares, the bottle, the pills. When he finished, the pastor handed him a small pamphlet and said, "There's a program at the mission downtown. Men who've seen what you've seen, who've carried what you carry. It's not easy, but it's a start." Jacob accepted it, not sure he believed in healing, but willing to try.

At his first meeting, he sat in a circle of worn chairs, faces lined with pain and understanding. He didn't speak that night, only listened—to stories of broken families, sleepless nights, and battles that never ended even after the war was done. When the meeting ended, he stepped outside into the crisp evening air, feeling both drained and strangely light.

As he turned toward the street, a voice called out behind him. "Jacob? Jake?" He froze. The voice was familiar, hesitant, disbelieving. Turning around, he saw a man walking toward him, limping slightly. It took him a moment to recognize him, but then the pieces fell into place. "Christopher?" The two men stood in stunned silence before pulling each other into an awkward embrace, the kind that spoke more than words could. They hadn't seen each other since the hospital. The memory of the explosion that tore their unit apart and decimated so much along the way came rushing right back to the forefront of Jacob's mind and filled him with a rush of anxiety.

They walked to a nearby coffee shop and sat for hours, nursing cups of black coffee that neither of them really tasted either. The conversation stumbled at first, small talk about how they'd ended up, how they'd survived, but soon the walls broke down. They spoke of Hank, the friend who hadn't made it, and the question that gnawed at them both: why him, and not us? "I see his face every night," Christopher confessed, staring into his cup. "Sometimes I still hear him laughing. Then I remember he's gone, and I wonder if I should've been the one instead." Jacob nodded slowly. "Yeah, I ask God the same thing. Feels like He's still deciding if I'm worth saving." Neither had an answer. They sat in silence, the hum of the café around them, two soldiers still trapped between past and present.

When Jacob finally returned to his motel room the quiet felt heavier than before. The half-empty bottle on the table seemed to watch him, daring him to pick it up. His hands shook. He thought of Maggie, of Ms. Goodchild, of the pastor's quiet prayer. Then almost as if surrendering, he reached for the small pill bottle instead. Swallowing one, then two, he lay back on the bed, eyes tracing the cracks in the ceiling as the morphine took hold. The pain dulled, the edges softened. His breath slowed. Sleep came at last, uneasy, but merciful.

Outside, the Missouri wind whispered against the motel window, carrying with it the faint echo of a promise not yet broken as Jacob fell into a deep, dream-filled state. Once again, there was water—a dream about water. Jacob's body tightened in his sleep as each gasp unfolded within his subconscious mind; he felt every drop of water as it glanced at his submerged body and heard the muted woosh of it as it plugged his ears. Usually calming, this scenario had the very liquid that sustains life, being the suffocating.

He was drowning, drowning in alcohol, drowning in self-pity, drowning in regret, drowning in trauma, drowning in guilt. He couldn't imagine going back to that church, that meeting room and facing the others who were trying their best to hang on. Nor could he envision looking Ms. Goodchild in her eyes and saying, "I give up, I surrender!" Jacob didn't want his family to be burdened by his eventual fallout. The weight of his struggles would be his and his alone in his mind. However, another tragic loss in their family would be heavier than he could grasp now.

Something woke him up, maybe it was his body telling him to breathe. He gasped for air; his eyes bore the weight of the world as he struggled to open them. Disoriented, he looked around the room amidst the predawn twilight drenched in sweat. His chest heaved as though he had been running for miles, his mind caught between dream and reality. The nightmares had returned, louder this time, more vivid. Hank's voice echoed in his head, the explosion replaying repeatedly, until Jacob could no longer tell if he was awake or still trapped in that day. His heart pounded. His hands trembled as he sat up on the edge of the bed, staring at the shadows cast by the faint light slipping through the blinds.

The world outside was still, the sky a deep indigo before the first blush of morning. Inside him, though, chaos raged. A heaviness pressed on his chest, the kind that made breathing itself feel like a burden. He ran his fingers through his hair, muttering, "I can't do this anymore," barely recognizing his own voice. He dressed in silence, buttoning his shirt with shaking fingers, and stepped out into the cool predawn air. The streets were empty, save for a few streetlamps casting long reflections on the damp pavement. He walked without thinking, guided by something between memory and despair, until he found himself near the river. The Mississippi rolled dark and wide before him, indifferent and eternal.

The Eads Bridge loomed ahead—iron and stone, its arches cutting through the early morning mist. He climbed its incline slowly, each step heavier than the last. The chill from the water below rose to meet him, and as he reached the midpoint, Jacob paused. He looked out over the river, its surface rippling with the faint light of dawn. For a long time, he simply stood there. His breath fogged in the cold air. He thought of Hank. Of Maggie's beauty and kindness. Of Miss Goodchild's faith. Of his father's despair. The weight of all of it pressed down until his knees weakened. *They'd be better off without me*, the thought whispered. *The world would be quieter without my noise.*

He gripped the rail, and his knuckles white. The current below seemed to call to him, promising rest, stillness, and ending to the ache. He closed his eyes. His whisper came out broken, almost inaudible. "God...I don't know how to do this anymore." His voice cracked, the words lost in the wind. Jacob looked out toward the horizon, streaks of pale gold cutting through the fog. He knew he'd miss some of the beautiful things this world had to offer like the majestic sky at sunrise and sunset, the laughter of his friends, the kind words of Ms. Goodchild, his family in their living room with a crackling fire with Mama and Papa and all his siblings under one roof, also Maggie's eyes, her brilliant blue eyes. He couldn't imagine living without all this but couldn't imagine living in the world he currently existed in with all this pain. He closed his eyes, exhaled and plunged forward off the bridge.

CHAPTER

11

"The Awakening"

Jacob's eyes suddenly opened and he couldn't believe what he was seeing. He remembered just moments before jumping off a bridge to end his life and now he appeared to be on some sort of beach. He seemed to be ok and not hurt, but he couldn't understand where he was, since his last memory was falling. He wasn't sure if he was dreaming or dead. As he cleared his focus and looked around, he began to see hundreds, maybe thousands of people all over the beach and in the water, but something seemed different. As he got closer, he saw a woman holding dead and dying children, and when he looked into the water, he saw lifeless bodies floating about.

As he approached the people, he heard them begging for water and pleading to save their kids. He wanted to help but he had no water. The people he saw looked diseased as if they hadn't eaten or had anything to drink for weeks. All around him he saw death. Jacob was so scared as he wasn't sure what was going on. He suddenly saw in the distance what appeared to be a man walking on the coastline towards him. Jake was frightened but saw that the man appeared to be healthy and given what he witnessed around him, he had a lot of questions. As Jacob got closer to the man, he asked the man what had happened here and why the man was not affected. In fact, Jacob was perplexed by what he saw and hoped this mysterious man could help him understand, as he only recalled moments before jumping from the bridge. The man had a very calming voice and put Jake at ease immediately. He introduced himself as Michael, and told Jacob that he was sent to meet and help him understand why he was there.

In fact, Jacob was given a great opportunity few were given to have the unseen and unknown explained in order to make changes in one's life. As well as to understand his purpose. Michael began to share the vision first by telling him a story where God put Abraham in a deep sleep state in order to share a vision of the future to help Abraham understand his calling of being a leader for many generations, even though he was without child at an old age, and that his wife, who was also beyond childbearing age, would miraculously bear a child. Michael began by stating what was told to Abraham by God.

"Do not be afraid, Abraham.
I am your shield,[a]
your very great reward.[b]"

[2] But Abraham said, "Sovereign LORD, what can you give me since I remain childless and the one who will inherit[c] my estate is Eliezer of Damascus?" [3] And Abraham said, "You have given me no children; so a servant in my household will be my heir."

[4] Then the word of the LORD came to him: "This man will not be your heir, but a son who is your own flesh and blood will be your heir." [5] He took him outside and said, "Look up at the sky and count

the stars—if indeed you can count them." Then he said to him, "So shall your offspring[d] be."

⁶ Abraham believed the Lord, and he credited it to him as righteousness.

⁷ He also said to him, "I am the Lord, who brought you out of Ur of the Chaldeans to give you this land to take possession of it."

⁸ But Abraham said, "Sovereign Lord, how can I know that I will gain possession of it?"

⁹ So the Lord said to him, "Bring me a heifer, a goat and a ram, each three years old, along with a dove and a young pigeon."

¹⁰ Abraham brought all these to him, cut them in two and arranged the halves opposite each other; the birds, however, he did not cut in half. ¹¹ Then birds of prey came down on the carcasses, but Abraham drove them away.

¹² As the sun was setting, Abraham fell into a deep sleep, and a thick and dreadful darkness came over him. ¹³ Then the Lord said to him, "Know for certain that for four hundred years your descendants will be strangers in a country not their own and that they will be enslaved and mistreated there. ¹⁴ But I will punish the nation they serve as slaves, and afterward they will come out with great possessions. ¹⁵ You, however, will go to your ancestors in peace and be buried at a good old age. ¹⁶ In the fourth generation your descendants will come back here, for the sin of the Amorites has not yet reached its full measure."

[17] When the sun had set and darkness had fallen, a smoking firepot with a blazing torch appeared and passed between the pieces. [18] On that day the LORD made a covenant with Abraham and said, "To your descendants I give this land, from the Wadi[e] of Egypt to the great river, the Euphrates— [19] the land of the Kenites, Kenizzites, Kadmonites, [20] Hittites, Perizzites, Rephaites, [21] Amorites, Canaanites, Girgashites and Jebusites."

Upon telling the story, Jacob asked about its significance and how it related to him. Michael informed him that God had watched and observed Jacob's life, and fully understood why he had fallen into despair to the point of jumping off the bridge in order to take his life. Jacob's breath was taken away and asked Michael how he knew that and why God would even allow such horrible things to occur in his life. Michael proceeded to tell Jacob another story to help him understand why God apparently allows bad things to happen in our lives so that he would understand how that related to him in his tragic journey.

Michael continued to tell the story of Abraham's great grandchild Joseph who had similar tragedy befall him, and how in his tragedy God was working on everything in the future to reveal the "why" of the tragedy, and like Joseph, Jacob would soon understand we can't always know the "why" in the moment. We have to believe that God who created us for a purpose, is working His purpose out in our circumstances, and revealing the reasons in His timing. Michael informed Jacob that God in fact, did give Abraham and his wife Sarah a child in the 90's and he had children who had children, one being Joseph.

Michael started the story by explaining that to Jacob; Abraham's grandson had multiple wives and multiple children by those wives but Jacob really only loved one which was Rachel, whom he had 2 children with, the first being Joseph, and then Benjamin before she died. Jacob loved Joseph so much and made him a special coat. Joseph had special gifts given to him by God that would later be used in the future. Joseph often had dreams of the future and what they meant. He then shared those with his brothers, and because of Jacob's love of Joseph and telling his brothers that in the future he would rule over them, his brothers were very jealous of him and despised him. They despised him so much they actually plotted to kill him. After speaking with one another, they decided to sell him into slavery and fake his death so their father would think he was dead. Joseph was sold into slavery by his brothers and sold to a leader in the Egyptian government. Because of Joseph's character he was given control over the man's whole household although still a slave.

Eventually, Joseph caught the eye of the wife of the owner who wanted Joseph for her very own. Joseph knew this was wrong and refused to comply with her sexual advances. Because he resisted, she falsely claimed he had raped her and was thrown into jail for many years. Even though falsely accused, Joseph was given favor while incarcerated,and was put in charge of the jail. Providentially, two men from the Pharaoh's court were accused of a crime against the Pharaoh and thrown into prison with Joseph. Both had dreams one night and shared them with the guards, who then told Joseph who could interpret the dreams. Joseph interpreted the dreams and told one he was going to be reinstated back to his position while the other was going to be sentenced to death.

Days later, Joseph's interpretations would come true. Joseph told the one who was saved that, if possible, please remember him in order to help him get out. Upon his release, the man Joseph saved forgot about Joseph until one day the Pharaoh had a dream which no one could translate. The man Joseph saved had then remembered him and told the Pharaoh his story and said that Joseph could interpret his dream. Joseph was called from Prison where the Pharaoh shared his dream and Joseph was able to interpret it and its meaning. Because of this the Pharaoh had pardoned Joseph from prison to put him in second of command over all of Egypt. What Joseph described in Pharaoh's dream was seven years of abundance and seven years of famine and the Pharaoh knew Joseph could help prepare Egypt for this.

Joseph set up places to store the abundance to help prepare for the time of famine. After seven years of abundance, the seven years of famine hit and many nations and countries were greatly impacted and came to Egypt for food which made Egypt very wealthy. Eventually Joseph's brothers came to Egypt for food and Joseph saw them, but he did not reveal himself to them. He plotted to get them accused of falsely stealing from him so that they would bring his brother Benjamin back to him. They were devastated, and their Father was heartbroken, as he didn't want to lose another son. They complied to the request and brought back their brother.

Upon their return, as they were certain they were going to be punished, Joseph revealed himself and forgave them and reminded them: "What you meant for evil—God meant for good." That which Joseph foretold his brothers many years ago became true so that God could save many from death. Upon completion of the story, Michael asked Jacob if understood its morals. Jacob stated he did, but he didn't understand how that related to him, and why he was there on that beach seeing all the dying people and what it meant. Michael began to explain to Jacob that God had a similar plan for him, as he did Joseph. Michael told Jacob that God had allowed all the tragedy in Jacob's life to prepare him for this revealed moment.

Michael asked Jacob if he had remembered what happened after his ship was destroyed, and if he had some type of vision and if so, what exactly was it. Jacob responded that he did remember and that he felt he should have died that day by drowning from going under and drinking sea water but he had not. He remembered how that impacted him, and knew that some day he was going to use that experience for good. Michael told Jacob today was that day. Jacob was confused, and asked Michael what he meant. Michael handed Jacob a piece of paper that said, "Your life mission is to take this information and turn salt water into drinking water." You will save millions, and you are to call this "The Water of Life." All who drink it will no longer thirst again. All these people you see here on this beach are dying of thirst, and they need you to save them. God has chosen you to save them much like he chose Abraham and Joseph, and many others. If you take up this call, you and those you touch will forever be blessed.

God has sent me to reveal your life calling and purpose for you to save others while sharing the lessons you have learned. Jacob fell on his knees and wept as he held Michael's hands, and thanked him. Michael helped Jacob up, and told him that he would be guiding him through his life. Jacob then turned around to look at all the people on the beach, and they were gone, as well as Michael. He then cried out and thanked God for what had happened.

The next thing Jacob hears is, "Clear," as he opens his eyes to realize that he is in an ambulance, and there are blurry visions of people who are tending to him. Then those miraculous words he'll never forget, "He is alive!"

CHAPTER

12

"Serendipity"

Jacob wasn't exactly sure where he was, but the stinging pain was a reminder that he was injured, but alive. He heard voices speaking and beeping noises around him. He tried opening his eyes, but even this was painful. Once he did, his vision was blurry. He opened his mouth to try and speak but had difficulty speaking. All of a sudden, he sensed someone near him but wasn't sure who it was except that she felt familiar. Upon hearing her voice, he knew immediately it was Maggie. He was barely able to speak her name but he did hear her say, Jacob " I am here, and will be here when you wake up."

Jacob drifted back to sleep due to the medication taking effect. As he dozed off he clearly remembered everything he had experienced previously with Michael and all those people on the beach. Several days later Jacob awoke to voices; they were stating that Jacob had attempted suicide by jumping off the bridge, and would have died had that boat not been nearby to rescue him. He also heard them say that he had suffered a concussion from hitting the water so hard, and several broken ribs, but that he would survive.

Jacob's voice was a little better and he immediately asked for Maggie. Maggie arrived shortly thereafter to tend to him. He thought he was dreaming, but soon found out that Maggie worked at the hospital, and by chance, he had come in the night of her shift and she stayed by his side the whole night. She had informed Jacob that she was now a nurse helping many of the previous soldiers who were struggling. He realized the odds of her working stateside in the exact place where he was recovering was more than just happenstance.

Jacob asked Maggie if they found a piece of paper on him with some instructions the day he was admitted, and she stated that there wasn't anything like that found. Jacob then proceeded to share with Maggie all that had happened since they last saw each other including his vision. Although Maggie had other patients to tend to, she kept coming back to spend time with Jacob, even after her shifts were over. In that very hospital room love began to bloom, and Maggie was captivated by Jacob's vision, and the purpose given to him.

Over the next month while in the hospital, they talked and planned for their life together, which included helping others. Maggie was fully committed to helping Jacob, even after all that had unfolded, she saw something special within his soul. Upon discharge, Jacob knew he had to go back home and see Ms. Goodchild, and Maggie requested time off to go with him. They made arrangements to go by train from St. Louis to his hometown, after having sent a wire ahead to alert Ms. Goodchild of his status, and that he would be coming home.

Ms. Goodchild went to town to run errands, stopped in and discovered there was a wire from Jacob. Her heart was set with praise and prayer as she fumbled to read. She hadn't seen him since he left for the war, and prayed the day he would come home safely. When she read that he was okay, just bruised up, her heart leapt for joy, and also shed tears of joy, immediately followed by a sense of concern for what he may have been suffering through. Jacob wrote, "that he had so much to share once home, as well as a huge surprise for her." She hurriedly raced home to prepare for his homecoming. She immediately praised God for watching over Jacob during this time, and also reached out to all the family about Jacob's return.

Several days later, Maggie and Jacob arrived home to find the entire family there to greet him, and celebrate his homecoming. Jacob spent the next several hours sharing with his family all that had happened during the war, and how he was one of the few survivors. He shared his depression, homelessness, addictions and attempted suicide, and how God had delivered him taking his own life. He wasn't ready to share with the others his vision as he wasn't sure what they would think. His brothers ands sisters shared updates on their lives, and for the first time in a long time it really felt like the family was whole again. After dinner, Jacob took Maggie out for a walk and under the moonlight, they paused to see a shooting star, and held Maggie's hands and softly kissed her under the moonlight, and proceeded to ask her to marry him, and she accepted.

They immediately went in to the house to tell Ms. Goodchild who was absolutely overjoyed for both of them. Ms. Goodchild then clasped each of their hands and prayed a blessing over them. Both could feel the power of God with this blessing. After the prayer, Jacob felt compelled to share his vision with Ms. Goodchild and he began sharing with her what had happened after he jumped off the bridge; how he was suddenly transported to a beach where so many people were suffering and dying. He continued explaining how he met a man named Micheal and the stories this man shared with him about Abraham and Joseph, as well as how Michael told Jacob what his purpose was.

Ms. Good child was listening with her hand over her mouth as she gasped, and proceeded to tell Jacob that she had a similar vision for him while she was dreaming several weeks before. She then stated that she was visited by a man named Michael in her vision who told her she was to help Jacob fulfill God's plans for him. Ms.Goodchild knew with all her heart that God had blessed them with oil on their land which saved the family home, farm, and the resources to take care of all of their needs, as well as the capital to fuel his project. They all wept and rejoiced that God had called them to such a great mission. The rest of the night Ms. Goodchild shared many bible verses and stories— reminders of God's will to fulfill their calling in their lives.

CHAPTER

13

"A Real-life Mission"

The next morning the house was buzzing with plans for Jacob and Maggie to wed and Jacob to start his new venture with Maggie. They spent the next two weeks planning, meeting with Maggie's parents, and family. They decided to set the wedding for Valentine's Day, six months after Jacob had asked Maggie to marry him. They chose to marry at the farm with the whole town invited.

Jacob told his family he was going into business for himself, but was hesitant to tell everyone the details, as he didn't want anyone to think he had lost his mind. No one would believe that he had a vision and, in that vision, he was given the recipe of how to turn salt water into drinking water. The only ones who knew were Maggie and Ms. Goodchild.

After Maggie and Jacob married, they went to work with Ms. Goodchild making God's vision come to fruition. Ms. Goodchild shared with Jacob while he was away at war, that God had helped to save their farm. She explained how she hired a geologist to check the land for minerals or anything of value within their land. Surprisingly, he informed her that the farm was rich with oil. After doing a thorough investigation they had discovered oil reserves that were worth hundreds of thousands of dollars, maybe millions.

Ms. Goodchild then set up monies for each of the children to help them with their dreams and goals. Also, when she had the vision, it became clear what she was to do for Jacob's dream. She informed that Jacob had over $100,000 for Maggie and him to invest in his project. They then proceeded to go to work on gathering the things needed to turn salt water into drinking water. They then hired the necessary crew including biologists, chemists, and scientists who specialized in water filtration.

Although Jacob didn't have the paper with the instructions, they were downloaded to his brain, and his team went to work on following the formula. During the next year, they continued on making the impossible possible. They kept their experiments under wraps for fear of theft. They knew what they were working and if they fell into the wrong hands, it could be devastating. Jacob kept his vision of all those dying people at the forefront of his mind.

During that year of perfecting the formula, and widespread manufacturing and distribution, Jacob and Maggie took the time to travel to Africa. It was there they realized what impact the water would have on populations of those who did not have running water. When they arrived in Ethiopia and Liberia, they were shocked at how many people were dying of disease due to lack of clean water.

Upon their return, they both had a renewed vision of making Water of Life a reality. On their second anniversary, their dream had become a reality and they successfully turned salt water into drinking water. It wasn't just drinking water, it was water like none other. Many would say that it was more than just thirst-quenching, it was like drinking living water, and they exulted in joy as they knew they would never thirst again!

When Jacob successfully fulfilled his vision with *The Water of Life*, Ms. Goodchild gathered all around and told the story of when Jesus met the Samaritan woman at the well, (John chapter 4) to explain how he wanted to give her and others water they had never had, which would make them never thirst again. She explained that the water he offered was himself, and if they had him, all their needs would be met. She used this story to help them remember that God gave Jacob this formula to help millions of others, not only to be able to have clean water, but to remember that God loves them, and that ultimately what they desire is found in Him.

Ms. Goodchild never wanted Jacob or others to forget that all we have comes from God and we are just stewards of his gifts.

[7-8] A woman, a Samaritan, came to draw water. Jesus said, "Would you give me a drink of water?" (His disciples had gone to the village to buy food for lunch.)

[9] The Samaritan woman, taken aback, asked, "How come you, a Jew, are asking me, a Samaritan woman, for a drink?" (Jews in those days wouldn't be caught dead talking to Samaritans.)

[10] Jesus answered, "If you knew the generosity of God and who I am, you would be asking *me* for a drink, and I would give you fresh, living water."

[11-12] The woman said, "Sir, you don't even have a bucket to draw with, and this well is deep. So how are you going to get this 'living water'? Are you a better man than our ancestor Jacob, who dug this well and drank from it, he and his sons and livestock, and passed it down to us?"

[13-14] Jesus said, "Everyone who drinks this water will get thirsty again and again. Anyone who drinks the water I give will never thirst—not ever. The water I give will be an artesian spring within, gushing fountains of endless life."

[15] The woman said, "Sir, give me this water so I won't ever get thirsty, won't ever have to come back to this well again!"

After her story and explanation, all understood and they spent the next hour just praying God would bless their efforts. After the formula was a success, they proceeded to secure it so that it could never be stolen or replicated by others for the wrong purposes. They also secured the necessary resources for large production and distribution. Jacob prayed God would protect him and Maggie and would place on His team both men and women of integrity and character to sit on his board for safeguarding purposes.

Once they secured everything they needed for production and distribution, they set up a meeting with their senator, as they knew there would be political ramifications across the globe. With the war having come to a close, and a new President, there was much work ahead needed to restore the world from the devastation of war. A meeting was set up with Senator Briggs, who had replaced Truman when he became President. The meeting took place April 16 1945,and Jacob shared with Senator Briggs what he had discovered, and its impact worldwide. Jacob wanted to ensure the Senator understood what his world vision was and the vitality to share it. Jacob also wanted to make sure he had the protection of the government for distribution.

Upon the conclusion of this meeting, Senator Briggs conferred with the President as to what could be expected next. The president requested to meet with Jacob, but due to post war issues, the meeting didn't take place until late 1946 when the president was sent to the Keys due to health. During 1945 and 1946 Jacob and Maggie met with many companies and businesses to discuss how his invention was going to help others. During this time Jacob met with several notaries such as John D. Rockefeller, who was fully behind Jacob and captured his vision of a world where clean water would be available to all.

CHAPTER

14

"President Truman"

It was December 12th 1946 when Maggie answered the phone to which the operator stated that the call was from The White House and they requested to speak to Jacob. Maggie immediately grabbed Jacob and told him and handed him the phone while whispering anxiously, "It's the White House on the phone for you!" The gentlemen stated he was James Byrne, President Truman's Secretary Of State, and that he and President Truman wanted to meet with Jacob about his invention.

They proceeded to schedule a meeting for January 1947 in the Florida Keys where President Truman was visiting for health reasons, while this location was temporarily being used for a satellite office of The White House. Maggie and Jacob were beyond thrilled, not only because of the opportunity to meet the President but they were expecting their first child in 1947.

It was January 27th and Jacob was sitting in a room waiting to meet with President Truman. Shortly after Secretary of State Byrne came for Jacob and brought him to meet the president. When Jacob was escorted to meet with President Truman, he was offered some of Truman's favorite Bourbon. The men discussed the war while Jacob shared his story to Mr. Truman, who was fascinated by it. The story eventually unfolded to Jacob's invention as he felt comfortable sharing with the President his vision knowing he was a very religious man and would understand.

President Truman was raised Baptist and followed the teaching of the scripture. The president was amazed at Jacobs' story, and could relate to him being called to do something great as he too, felt the same calling on his life to handle a post war world. Both men hit it off well, and President Truman was committed to helping Jacob with his vision, as he felt his company "Water of Life" could play a vital role in healing and helping in post war recovery. Mr. Truman spoke with the Secretary of State to make arrangements to have Jacob's company secure contracts across the world to provide drinking water to help those throughout the globe.

Jacob took the opportunity to talk with the President about the war and what led up to its magnitude. President Truman then began to discuss with Jacob the history behind the rise of Hitler and Mussolini and their Ideology of Nazism and fascism. Both men were dictators who wanted to dominate and control the world with ideology. President Truman stated that the war came down to world dominance or good versus evil. The allies were for freedom while Hitler, Mussolini, and the Japanese were for control and domination. The allies wanted to ensure the world had freedom as outlined in the constitution as formed by our Founding Fathers, based on interpretation from scriptures. President Truman gave Jacob a basic instruction of the enemy's ideology and how important it was to safeguard against this their tyrannical intentions.

President Truman laid out the fundamental differences of the enemy's ideology of Nazism, Fascism, Communism, and Socialism. versus America's. He stated that America was formed with an ideology based on freedom and democracy not government control or totalitarianism. America's democracy and form of government as developed by the founding Fathers came directly from scripture to ensure man's rights were protected. Truman warned if the enemy's ideologies take hold in America, then America as we know it, will cease to exist. Truman then proceeded to educate Jacob on these ideologies and the natural outworking and destruction when implemented. Using the example of how Nazism was used for the horrific attempts to annihilate the Jewish population.

He explained the inner-workings and infrastructure of **fascism**, **communism, Nazism** and **Socialism** when describing an overcontrolling government. President Truman stated that they were different from a democratic government as well as a capitalistic economy, but they are also different from each other. He asked Jacob if he knew what Fas**cism was, to which Jacob stated he had heard of it, but wasn't clear how it played out within the government. Mr.Truman continued explaining how f**ascism is a government system led by one person, a dictator, who has complete power over the country. It's also known as a totalitarian government. Citizens of fascist countries must surrender their individual liberties and pledge extreme allegiance to their leader. Its origins started with Benito Mussolini who, aligned with Hitler, created the one-party fascist state in post-World War I Italy.

Nazism was similar, and a combination or form of fascism as well as Socialism. Its principles included: a disdain for liberal democracy, and the Parliamentary system. Its beliefs include support for dictatorship, antisemitism, white supremacy, and social Darwinism. Nazism sought to overcome social divisions and create a homogeneous German society based on "racial purity." The Nazis aimed to unite all Germans living in historically German territory, gain lands for expansion and expand the idea of Natural Socialism. This arose from attempts to create a nationalist redefinition of socialism. Truman stated that Hitler wanted world domination, and a destruction of freedom. Truman elaborated on some of the differences between Nazism and Fascism. He shared Fascism's principles on the following points:

- *Anti-Neutralism - Fascists do not believe in seeing "both sides" or staying neutral; you're either with them or against them.*

- *Anti-Union - Labor unions are illegal in fascist nations, and are replaced by government-controlled labor organizations.*

- *Autarky (economic self-sufficiency) - Fascist countries reject both economic socialism and the free market of capitalism and prefer to be completely self-sufficient without relying on other nations.*

- *Economic Regulation - The government controls economic activity. It allows private profit — as long as that profit benefits the state.*

- *Far-Right Ideology - Fascism falls on the far right side of the political spectrum, favoring racial purity, religious fundamentalism and limited personal freedom.*

- *Nationalism - Citizens must put the country before their own interests, and the nation puts its own needs before all other nations.*

- *Social Hierarchy - Those in a fascist nation don't believe in equality. They believe that class conflict is important to maintaining order in the nation.*

- *Strength - Fascist governments are militaristic, and they use violence and brutality to demonstrate their strength on the world stage.*

- *Victimhood - The country sees itself as a victim of other nations' cruelty. It believes that it can do whatever is necessary to right the wrongs done by other nations.*

Truman then asked Jacob if he had heard of Communism. Jacob stated that he thought it was similar, and found in places like Russia. The President explained that unlike fascism, a communist government focuses on equal treatment and opportunities for all citizens. It opposes capitalism which encourages private profit and the empowerment of the individual. The philosophy of communism includes spreading its influence across country borders.

Its origins began with the concept of an egalitarian society without classes or economic privilege, and had its roots in ancient Greece, The European Renaissance, and the Age of Enlightenment. However, it was Karl Marx and Friedrich Engels who defined modern communism in their 1848 pamphlet *The Communist Manifesto*. In one of the most famous examples of communism was Vladimir Lenin's Bolshevik party which took control of Russia in the 1917 Bolshevik Revolution. Truman then explained the p**rinciples of Communism:**

The most basic tenet of communism indicates that workers who are responsible for producing wealth should have a share of that wealth. But there are more important principles in a communist government, including:

- *Anti-Capitalism - In communist governments and economies, there is no free market or private profit. Communists reject what they perceive as selfishness and greed in capitalism.*

- ***Anti-Religion*** - Marx regarded organized religion as "the opium of the people" because it prompts workers to accept capitalist oppression as part of their god's plan.

- ***Authoritarianism*** - The first phase of a communist state is the revolution, followed by a period of authoritarian control (phase 2) before surrendering control to the people (phase 3). However, no modern communist state has been able to move from phase 2 into phase 3, as leaders have held on to their control.

- ***Classlessness*** - Communists believe in a society that doesn't have social or economic class divisions (such as bourgeoisie vs. proletariat). The state is run by members of the working class in the interest of the working class.

- ***Collectivism*** - Communist countries demand that all property is turned over to the state to be shared with all citizens.

- ***Government Control*** - Communists believe that the government must intervene heavily in citizens' lives to keep them from achieving more than others. This includes control over education, employment and even marriage and family.

- ***Far-Left Ideology, Far-Right Tactics*** - The concepts of social equality and sharing resources are a fundamental part of far-left ideology. However, the modern implementation of communism, including authoritarianism and limiting individual freedom, are closer to the right side of the political spectrum.

- ***International Influence*** - Communism is meant to be spread across the globe, not controlled within a country's borders.

- ***Revolution*** - In order to achieve a communist utopia, the communist party must revolt against the ruling class — violently, if necessary. While some communists believe in reforming an existing government, most think that the entire structure must be overthrown and started again.

Finally Truman went on to explain what Socialism was. He stated that many people believe that socialism and communism are basically the same thing. While communism is a form of socialism, the two government systems are quite different in practice. Socialism can co-exist with capitalism, unlike communism, and does in most modern democracies (known as democratic socialism). He then went onto explain the principles *of socialism:*

- **Central Planning -** *Purely socialist governments intervene in economic activity, rather than trust the "invisible hand" of the free market. This includes government-owned companies and price regulation by bureaucrats.*

- *Collective Ownership - Also known as "social" or "common" ownership, this principle contends that the factors of production (labor, goods, natural resources) should be owned by all members of a society.*

- *Cooperation over Competition - Socialists reject the competitive nature of capitalism. They embrace egalitarianism as the ideal way to ensure social stability.*

- *Distribution of Wealth - Socialist societies have high tax rates that are redistributed into government programs and infrastructure. It relates to Marx's quote: "From each according to ability, to each according to need."*

- *Equality of Opportunity - Socialism embraces the concept of social equality and fairness. It works to eliminate social and economic barriers based on prejudice or lack of access.*

- *Far-Left Ideology - Socialism can be as far left on the political spectrum as fascism is far right. Advocates of socialism often believe in the elimination of private property, a strongly regulated economy and well-funded government programs.*

- *Protecting the Oppressed - The principle of protecting those oppressed by other is seen as a responsibility of government. Examples of government programs aimed to help underserved members of society include universal healthcare and welfare programs.*

- *Separation of Church and State - Socialists support religious freedom but do not believe in a relationship between the state and any religion in particular.*

- *Workers' Rights - Like communists, socialists support workers' rights. But instead of a workers' revolution, socialists advocate for labor unions and workplace regulations.*

After President Truman concluded his lesson on various failed governmental ideologies Jacob was absolutely amazed at the lesson he was taught. President Truman then shared a story from the Old Testament out of Judges 2 to hammer home his point. Truman informed Jacob that the Israelites entered the promised land and after one generation they had forgotten God and their deliverance because they allowed the ideology of others who did not possess the knowledge of the truth to take the minds captive. Here is the story Truman shared with Jacob out of Judges 2:

"The angel of the LORD went up from Gilgal to Bokim and said, "I brought you up out of Egypt and led you into the land I swore to give to your ancestors. I said, 'I will never break my covenant with you, ² and you shall not make a covenant with the people of this land, but you shall break down their altars.' Yet you have disobeyed me. Why have you done

this? ³ And I have also said, 'I will not drive them out before you; they will become traps for you, and their gods will become snares to you.'"

⁴ When the angel of the LORD had spoken these things to all the Israelites, the people wept aloud, ⁵ and they called that place Bokim.[a] There they offered sacrifices to the LORD.

⁶ After Joshua had dismissed the Israelites, they went to take possession of the land, each to their own inheritance. ⁷ The people served the LORD throughout the lifetime of Joshua and of the elders who outlived him and who had seen all the great things the LORD had done for Israel.

⁸ Joshua son of Nun, the servant of the LORD, died at the age of a hundred and ten. ⁹ And they buried him in the land of his inheritance, at Timnath Heres[b] in the hill country of Ephraim, north of Mount Gaash.

¹⁰ After that whole generation had been gathered to their ancestors, another generation grew up who knew neither the LORD nor what he had done for Israel. ¹¹ Then the Israelites did evil in the eyes of the LORD and served the Baals. ¹² They forsook the LORD, the God of their ancestors, who had brought them out of Egypt. They followed and worshiped various gods of the peoples around them. They aroused the LORD's anger ¹³ because they forsook him and served Baal and the Ashtoreths. ¹⁴ In his anger against Israel the LORD gave them into the hands of raiders who plundered them. He sold them into the hands of their enemies all around, whom they were no longer able to resist. ¹⁵ Whenever Israel went out to fight, the hand of the LORD was against them to defeat them, just as he had sworn to them. They were in great distress.

[16] Then the LORD raised up judges,[c] who saved them out of the hands of these raiders. [17] Yet they would not listen to their judges but prostituted themselves to other gods and worshiped them. They quickly turned from the ways of their ancestors, who had been obedient to the LORD's commands. [18] Whenever the LORD raised up a judge for them, he was with the judge and saved them out of the hands of their enemies as long as the judge lived; for the LORD relented because of their groaning under those who oppressed and afflicted them. [19] But when the judge died, the people returned to ways even more corrupt than those of their ancestors, following other gods and serving and worshiping them. They refused to give up their evil practices and stubborn ways.

[20] Therefore the LORD was very angry with Israel and said, "Because this nation has violated the covenant I ordained for their ancestors and has not listened to me, [21] I will no longer drive out before them any of the nations Joshua left when he died. [22] I will use them to test Israel and see whether they will keep the way of the LORD and walk in it as their ancestors did." [23] The LORD had allowed those nations to remain; he did not drive them out at once by giving them into the hands of Joshua."

President Truman reminded Jacob that the United States was a blessed nation because it was established on Godly principles and if America ever abandons those principles to other ideologies such as Nazism, fascism, communism, or socialism then we would lose our blessings. Jacob thanked the President for his wisdom and counsel and told the president if there was any way he could serve then he would be willing to help in any way. Jacob and the President then shared a prayer before heading out.

CHAPTER

15

"The Marshall Plan"

Later that year Maggie and Jacob had their first child, which they named Michael after the man in the vision. They ended up settling in upstate NY living in Saratoga near Lake George. They soon found out after Micheal was born that Maggie was expecting a second child to be born the following year. Because of the business taking off and his commitment to President Truman to assist with the implementation of the Marshal plan Jacob was traveling overseas quite a bit. Because of the kids and the new baby they asked if Ms. Goodchild could move in to help Maggie which she graciously accepts.

Within five years of developing the formula they had multiple plants on each coast of the US and in Europe. Water of life industries were known all over the world with the help of President Truman and Rockefeller advocating and getting behind Jacob's vision. Jacob was assisting in the implementation of the Marshall Plan named after Secretary of State George Marshall to help rebuild the western European economies. He was meeting with leaders such as Winston Churchill and Gandhi.

In 1947, Jacob was visiting India and Africa, he had the opportunity to meet Mahatma Gandhi and better understand the needs in his country and Gandhi's vision of independence. Gandhi shared with Jacob the sacrifices he had made for freedom for his people and how he was able to fight for the cause of his people. Jacob had learned a tremendous amount from Gandhi on leading others and what mattered most.

During that time and the next 10 years Jacob meets with world leaders to help discover how they could work together to address the world's needs related to providing drinking water to those who didn't have access to fresh water. During his travels Jacob was able to see so much suffering that reminded him of his vision years ago and used that vision to compel him to work with leaders to come up with technology and equipment to provide drinking water in the remotest places. During the next five years He and Maggie had a total of 5 kids Michael, Rachel, Elijah, Emily and Joseph. Life couldn't have been better for Jacob and Maggie and their Family. Water of Life industries was now producing drinkable water filtered from salt water all over the world and was making an impact on the world and saving lives in the remotest places.

While Jacob was in NY at a board meeting Jacob ran into an old friend from the war, Chris. After his meeting the two met for dinner and reviewed the last few years and Chris couldn't believe all that happened to Jacob. Chris shared with Jacob some of his struggles with Jacob especially about being unemployed. Jacob had compassion for Chris and hired him on the spot. Chris ended up working in the NY office and quickly learned the business and became pretty close to Jacob during the next few years. Jacobs was thrilled how well Chris was doing and began to trust Chris with much of the business decisions as Jacob spent time on international affairs and with Family.

Maggie was happy for Jacob but had some reservations regarding Chris and tried to express her concerns to Jacob. Jacob would repeatedly tell her he was an old war buddy and was there for Jacob back then. One Sunday morning there were missionaries attending their church who spoke of how life was in the jungles of Africa and their plea for others to come and help.

As Jacob and Maggie were sharing lunch, they spoke about the vision God showed Jacob years earlier and what they could do now to help. Although they had been faithful with what God revealed to them and being obedient in creating the formula they felt God had a greater calling on their life to make a difference. The company was doing well and they were making millions providing drinking water across the globe but they began to ask what else they could do.

Both made the decision they would take their family on a trip around the globe not necessarily to see the world and experience what the world had to offer but to see how they could see what the world's needs were and how they could make a difference. It was now 1960 and a new President (Kennedy) was elected whom Jacob and Maggie got to meet at his inauguration. Jacob decided to give Chris more control over the company and put him in charge over the next year while they were on their trip. Later that year they started their one-year trip around the world. The goal was not only to see the many parts of the world but to allow God to guide them in opening their eyes to the needs of the world around them.

CHAPTER

16

"The Betrayal"

They were well into their trip around the world, visiting several countries including China, Africa, South America, Italy and Spain. For Jacob and his family, it wasn't just a year of vacationing, but more of a world-wide mission trip. It was important for both Maggie and Jacob's children to experience the world and see what others had to experience and endure, while discovering what were their greatest needs too.

Ms. Goodchild played a vital role in helping form the moral character of the kids, while ensuring they were taught well while on the year long journey. They immersed themselves in the culture while interacting with people from all walks of life. They couldn't help but be fascinated by how unique everyone they met was. Jacob was reminded of what Truman had taught him years ago about certain ideologies prescribed in certain countries and how that played out amongst the people of those countries, as well as how appreciative he was where he was from.

The kids began learning different languages such as Spanish, French, Portuguese, Italian, and Chinese. They also got to experience different foods that were unique to those regions. Their favorites were "Spanish" dishes from Guatemala and Costa Rica, as well as those from Italy. They all loved going to Rome where they were able to meet Pope John XXIII. He gave them a personal tour of the Vatican and St. Peter's Cathedral. And while they were there, Jacob had a private meeting with the Pope about the greatest area of needs amongst them for the "Water of Life" that Jacob's company could fulfill.

The Pope himself was very appreciative of Jacob and his calling to help provide water to the world. Jacob had the honor of sharing his vision with the Pope and was deeply grateful that the supreme pontiff prayed a blessing over Jacob and his entire family upon their departure. Prior to leaving Rome Jacob fell into a deep sleep and had another vision. In this vision he was once again on a beach in the midst of a storm. He could barely see, but he witnessed a man within the storm approaching him, and soon realized it was Michael from his first vision long ago.

As Michael approached Jacob, he looked concerned. Jacob embraced Michael and asked him what was going on and why he was there. Michael explained that he was always with Jacob and was so proud he had been faithful to his vision, but things were in jeopardy and that Michael had been sent to warn him. Michael explained to Jacob that sometimes people we think we can trust aren't who we thought they were and often they are sheep in wolf's clothing. Michael went on to share a story of the man who betrayed Jesus. He said his name was Judas and explained what happened that led to the betrayal.

"I do not speak concerning all of you. I know whom I have chosen; but that the Scripture may be fulfilled, 'He who eats [a]bread with Me has lifted up his heel against Me.' 19 Now I tell you before it comes, that when it does come to pass, you may believe that I am He. 20 Most assuredly, I say to you, he who receives whomever I send receives Me; and he who receives Me receives Him who sent Me. 21 When Jesus had said these things, He was troubled in spirit, and testified and said, "Most assuredly, I say to you, one of you will betray Me." 22 Then the disciples looked at one another, perplexed about whom He spoke.

23 Now there was [b]leaning on Jesus' bosom one of His disciples, whom Jesus loved. 24 Simon Peter therefore motioned to him to ask who it was of whom He spoke. 25 Then, leaning [c]back on Jesus' breast, he said to Him, "Lord, who is it? 26 Jesus answered, "It is he to whom I shall give a piece of bread when I have dipped it." And having dipped the bread, He gave it to Judas Iscariot, the son of Simon. 27 Now after the piece of bread, Satan entered him. Then Jesus said to him, "What you do, do quickly." 28 But no one at the table knew for what reason He said this to him. 29 For some thought, because Judas had the money box, that Jesus had said to him, "Buy those things we need for the feast," or that he should give something to the poor. Now the Festival of Unleavened Bread, called the Passover, was approaching, 2 and the chief priests and the teachers of the law were looking for some way to get rid of Jesus, for they were afraid of the people. 3 Then Satan entered Judas, called Iscariot, one of the Twelve. 4 And Judas went to the chief priests and the officers of the temple guard and discussed with them how he might betray Jesus. 5 They were delighted and agreed to give him money. 6 He consented, and watched for an opportunity to hand Jesus over to them when no crowd was present. And while He was still speaking, behold, Judas, one of the twelve, with a great multitude with swords and clubs, came from the chief priests and elders of the people.

[48] Now His betrayer had given them a sign, saying, "Whomever I kiss, He is the One; seize Him." [49] Immediately he went up to Jesus and said, "Greetings, Rabbi!" and kissed Him.

Michael then explained to Jacob that he had a betrayer in his midst who was trying to steal his vision and all that he loved. Jacob asked Michael who it was and what he needed to do. Michael then revealed to Jacob that it was Chris who was plotting to take over the company and remove Jacob as the Chairman. Michael informed Jacob of what was going on and directed him to return to his office in New York immediately, and that the board was meeting in the upcoming week to discharge Jacob based on false allegations Chris had made.

Jacob then awoke from his dream and immediately told Maggie and Ms. Goodchild of his vision. Jacob reached out to one of his closest associates and confirmed the board was meeting. Jacob told them about his vision and asked that his friend look into it. Shortly thereafter, his friend was able to confirm the vision. Jacob then made arrangements to immediately return and attend the board meeting.

When Jacob returned to New York there was an anonymous envelope with the evidence Jacob needed of Chris's betrayal. Exactly one week after the vision, the board was meeting to hear Chris's complaint against Jacob and request his termination as Chairman. Suddenly Jacob walks in and Chris approaches him with a hug and kiss on the cheek. Jacob pauses for a moment and reflects on that and the story Michael had shared about Jesus' betrayal. Jacob then proceeds to lay out the evidence against Chris and previously arranges for the police to remove him, and subsequently escorted Chris out in handcuffs.

The board was in shock and profusely apologized to Jacob while informing him they had all been deceived by Chris. After Jacob removed Chris, he discovered that he had embezzled millions from "Water Of Life," and had seriously tarnished Jacob's work. Jacob Steele and the board spent the next year working with their shareholders and offices to undo the damage Chris had done while reestablishing their good name.

One night Jacob and Maggie reflected on the lessons from the betrayal, and how Jacob was blind to Chris's deceit. Maggie told Jacob that even with Judas' betrayal of Jesus there was a reason and purpose behind it, and God was teaching Jacob a valuable lesson in the warning. Jacob recognized that the vision God gave him was for Jacob, and that he needed to be a good and faithful steward of that vision while using wisdom and discernment in who he trusts to join in the implementation of the vision.

CHAPTER

17

"The Changing Times"

It was November 22, 1963 and Jacob had just finished his jog and as he turned on the radio, he paused for a moment to try and process what he was hearing; President John F. Kennedy had just been assassinated. He stood there in shock as he recalled having met with President Kennedy just months before in the oval office discussing the needs of victims who lacked fresh water from the devastation of hurricane Flora.

Jacob knew that the president had some enemies from the Cuban Missile Crisis. He was also fully aware of the growing issues from the Vietnam War taking place. Water of Life was back where it needed to be serving humanity on a global scale. Jacob had trained Michael and implemented him as CEO while he focused more on the humanitarian needs around the world. Jacob was concerned about the unrest throughout the world, but especially in the U.S. Five short years after the JFK assassination, Dr. Martin Luther King, the courageous and peaceful civil rights leader, was assassinated on April 4, 1968, then two months later on June 5th, 1968 Bobby Kennedy was shot and killed at the Ambassador Hotel in Los Angeles shortly after midnight, after winning the California presidential primary.

Jacob had previously met both men at different times to discuss issues of civil rights and how to improve racial issues in the south. He remembered marching with Dr. King during the 1965 march from Selma to Montgomery. As things became more tumultuous during the 60's with unrest on college campuses, racial riots, the Vietnam war ramping up, Jacob noticed a dangerous ideology becoming very prevalent amongst the youth. It was a combination of radical left-wing ideology like communism, anarchism and the rise of anti-establishment sentiment. These radical movements were fueled by the civil rights struggle, and the Vietnam war. Jacob had once again remembered what Truman shared with him about dangerous ideologies and their impact on civilizations.

He also realized that in the early 60's there were some key court cases that removed teachings of the bible from schools as well as prayer. This concerned him, especially in light of the country's history of being Judeo Christian in its ideology. He remembered a quote from John Adams he once heard saying, "Our Constitution was made only for moral and religious people. It is wholly inadequate to the government of any other." As he traveled the world and began doing more humanitarian work, he had growing concerns that the evil ideology that led to Nazism and Fascism was beginning to creep into the US and schools, while basic morality was being dismissed which was going to deeply affect our world.

Later in 1969, both his boys Elijah and Joseph were drafted into the war and shipped off to Vietnam. Prior to their departure, the family prayed over both boys for God's protection over them. It would be the last time the boys would see their Grandmother Ms. Goodchild, as she passed away 6 months after they shipped out. Ms. Goodchild had taken ill in late 1968 due to a heart condition no one was aware of. She moved in with the Steele's that year as Maggie looked out for her. She was sent to the Lord on December 26, 1969 right after the family had celebrated Christmas. Both Maggie and Jacob were by her side when she passed.

Shortly into the new year of 1971 Jacob and Maggie received word that Joseph had been captured by the Vietnamese and was being held as a prisoner of war. Later that year, they received the unthinkable news that Elijah had been killed in combat. Both grieved the loss of their precious Elijah, and reflected on the precious times they had with him as they held a celebration of life with the family.

It was 1973 when a landmark case went to the Supreme Court that greatly impacted Jacob and the world. The Supreme Court made the decision to legalize abortion in the first trimester of pregnancy. Jacob thought to himself and remembered hearing that almost 3 million Jews were killed by Hitler's tyranny. He could almost imagine how many innocent babies were going to be killed because of this decision (Jacob couldn't even imagine that at the time of his death almost 63 million babies would be killed because of this decision). He knew within the depths of his soul that this decision was birthed out of evil, and that was a direct correlation to a removal of bible teachings of morality from schools and government and clothed within the lie of "a woman's right to choose because it's her own body." He could not believe that we, as a country, had come to this point where we would allow the killing of innocent children which was no less of an atrocity as the killing of the Jews in his mind.

Later that year, they received word that Joseph had been released and would soon be returning home. He arrived home a month earlier where the family gratefully celebrated his arrival. It was a blessing to have him home, but they soon realized that he was suffering PTSD from his prisoner of war experience and would need a lot of love and support. Jacob spent a lot of time with Joseph to help him recover from his traumatic experience as a P.O.W. Jacob and Maggie soon became grandparents as Michael and his wife Rebecca had their first child. As the years progressed, Michael and Rebecca had other children, in addition to their daughters Rachel and Emily, who both married well to wonderful men.

The Steele family continued to count their blessings and Jacob"s Water of Life Company was doing better than ever. It was 1982 and Jacob was invited to the White House where he was to receive the Presidential Medal of Freedom from President Ronald Reagan. This award was the highest civilian honor given to a citizen. Jacob and President Reagan hit it off from the very beginning and spent many times together consulting on government affairs. Jacob shared his stories with President Reagan about his visits in the "Little White House" with President Truman, and all that he had learned from him. He told him about being involved in the rebuilding of Europe under the Marshall plan, meeting Churchill and Gandhi too. Both had long discussions about the state of the world, and Jacob shared his personal inner struggles with the killing of the unborn, which also greatly troubled Reagan. Many times they would pray together that God would guide them and ultimately His will would be served through both men. Jacob really admired Reagan's strength and leadership, including how well he was at working with others who differed from him. Jacob learned from Reagan how one could work with others in their differences without compromising their integrity and beliefs. Many times, Maggie and Jacob were invited to Reagan's ranch for horseback riding. They remained friends even after he left office.

CHAPTER

18

"The Close of a Century"

It was December 31ˢᵗ 1999 and Jacob was 75 years old, enjoying a fulfilling and blessed existence while celebrating the last day of the year and century with the love of his life, Maggie. They were both reflecting on their 54 years together and how absolutely blessed they had been. They thought about God and how He had given them so much, as well as how they tried to be good stewards of His gifts. Both took stock of all they had in their lives and how God had blessed Water of Life Industries too. Jacob had largely turned over control to Michael who had helped catapult Water of Life's revenue to half a Trillion and was actively being traded on Wall Street.

Jacob and Maggie were kept busy with humanitarian efforts all over the world including providing schools in countries that didn't have proper education, food to starving communities, assisting with the rescue of sex trafficked kids, on a global scale. There wasn't a cause or need that they weren't involved with. They started a nonprofit and foundation over 25 years ago that was supporting veterans, homeless, folks struggling with addiction, senior citizens, domestic violence victims, children who were at risk for abuse and neglect, individuals with mental health issues, as well as people with disabilities. The Steele's were extremely active working with their nonprofit and foundation both domestically and internationally.

One of the things they were especially proud of was that they were able to successfully collaborate with many other non-profits worldwide in helping bring a sense of unity and community to the greater cause of helping others. They were also directly involved within their church in spreading and bringing the community together to serve. While they were down working in Guatemala on a building program to house and educate abandoned kids, Maggie became very ill and feverish.

While Jacob was praying over Maggie, he fell into a deep sleep and had another vision; this time he was walking with Maggie hand in hand on the very beach he had envisioned before. They experienced an absolutely beautiful sunset as they walked, and once again, close by was a man who turned out to be Michael. As they approached, they embraced and Jacob introduced Maggie to Michael. A sense of peace filled them all and a relieved smile came upon Maggie's face as they heard a familiar and angelic voice speak, " Welcome, Maggie." It was Ms. Hannah Goodchild, and at that very moment both Jacob and Maggie knew they were safe.

As Michael looked at Jacob, a tear came down his cheek and he reminded him that the time had come for him to face one of the hardest journeys he would experience, but that he would be by his side, and that God never would abandon Him. Jacob didn't fully understand and told Michael that God gave him Maggie, and with her help, he could overcome every difficulty. Maggie then looked at Jacob and held him tight and began crying as she explained to him that her Earthly journey was over, and that he would have to go on without her. She told him that she would have to go with Michael and Ms. Goodchild now, but she would always be with Jacob, and they would soon be back together, to serve in eternity as they so faithfully served on earth.

Jacob then turned to Michael to ask why, and Michael stated that it was now time for Jacob to pass on all he had learned in the finding and fulfillment of his purpose to his children and their children while empowering the next generation. Micheal reminded Jacob of all the lessons he learned over the years, and that he had been a faithful servant to those in need, but it was now time to teach those lessons to others, as he eventually would be joining Maggie in eternity. His role and purpose now was to leave a legacy and teach others about God and His role in their lives in fulfilling their purpose to positively impact the world around them.

Michael explained to Jacob what he was to do and how he was to leave his mark before him until Maggie and he were together again. Jacob looked at Maggie, embraced her once more, before kissing her and saying goodbye to the love of his life, knowing deep in his heart it was only a temporary goodbye. Before she departed, Maggie said to Jacob, "Thank you for the life and love you gave me. I couldn't imagine living this life without you, and the heartfelt joy you provided each and every day." As Maggie turned to leave, Ms. Goodchild held her hand and walked with her.

Michael turned to Jacob and told him, "You have one more mission to fulfill before you come home." He stated that Jacob would be guided each and every day and that as long as he looked to God, he would know what to do and when to do it. Michael explained to him that this mission in some respects, was even greater than the first, in that the water he provided to others would only quench for the moment, but what he was going to do going forward would provide a light in the darkness for all to see. By helping others find their purpose he was going to connect them to their Creator who created them for a higher purpose. The very reason for their existence, which would meet their greatest need for love, peace and fulfillment.

Michael reminded Jacob how when he was at his lowest point at the bridge when he tried to throw his life away, and God revealed Jacob's purpose to him. When he obeyed and surrendered to God's purpose, Jacob's life was greatly blessed. Michael told Jacob to simply tell others what God had done for him. He reminded Jacob of the last words of Christ before his resurrection. It was called the great commission out of Matthew 28:

[16] Then the eleven disciples went to Galilee, to the mountain where Jesus had told them to go. [17] When they saw him, they worshiped him; but some doubted. [18] Then Jesus came to them and said, "All authority in heaven and on earth has been given to me. [19] Therefore go and make disciples of all nations, baptizing them in the name of the Father and of the Son and of the Holy Spirit, [20] and teaching them to obey everything I have commanded you. And surely I am with you always, to the very end of the age."

Michael reminded Jacob that he would always be there, and that God would never leave or forsake him whenever he needed him. When Jacob awakened, Maggie was gone. He was deeply saddened at the loss of his dearest Maggie, but He knew God had commissioned to fight the good fight and continue on his mission. He also knew that although Maggie was not going on with him, in this mission, she was always his inspiration and would be with him throughout. Jacob then made arrangements to have Maggie's body brought to the states for the funeral, where he would join his kids and grandkids for her services.

CHAPTER

19

"The New Mission"

After the funeral and several months of grieving over the loss of his beloved Maggie, Jacob decided to take a sabbatical for one year to try and completely understand his last vision and assignment. He chose a place in Italy that had deep and significant memories attached to it for he and Maggie. These were places that they both shared special moments, all while appreciating its rich history and beautiful scenery. He spent months in Rome, Amalfi, Capri and Venice during which he was able to spend time with the people and hear the needs amongst them.

He also spent extensive time in God's word and in prayer to best discern the next steps. After a year of travel and reflection, he reached out to various close friends to discuss his plan. He called a weekend meeting of world leaders and friends, many of whom were religious icons including Billy Graham, Rick Warren, Pope John Paul II and the Dalai Lama. As well as political leaders such as Tony Blair, George W. Bush, and Jacques Chirac from France. They were to meet at the

Grove Park Inn in Asheville. It was a secret meeting and many of the guests had to arrive at night through a hidden entrance so as to not alert publicity.

He especially liked The Grove Park Inn because Thomas Edison, Henry Ford, and Harvey Firestone had visited there in the past. Jacob greatly admired these men for their impact on society. It was April 21st 2002 when they met. As Jacob was heading down the halls looking at all the famous men and women who had been guests at the hotel, many whom he had met and known, his mind drifted to thoughts of Maggie, and he felt her presence with him in spirit as he was preparing for what he was going to share with his distinguished guests.

They congregated in the meeting room and all were anxious with excitement, as Jacob asked if he could open the meeting in prayer. After he thanked all who had come, he shared a little of his story and what he learned during his sabbatical. Jacob expressed concerns with the condition of the world, especially after all he had seen over his seventy seven years. He described the time he met with President Truman who explained all the events leading up to World War 2 and the lessons learned from that experience. Jacob reminded each of the guests, "That if we don't learn from history, we are doomed to repeat it." All while calling upon each person there, many of whom were world leaders, to use their platform responsibly for the betterment of this generation and the next so they can be better prepared for success.

He then continued by rolling out his plan of creating mentoring centers all over the world with an emphasis on the youth that would teach them a basis of morality, principles of truth and the distinction between right and wrong. Jacob believed strongly that because of dangers in ideology devoid of truth and morality, children would have no anchor to discern between good and evil. He also emphasized that these centers would not be allowed to teach indoctrination that has historically failed such as Fascism, Socialism, or Communism.

Additionally, he explained that these centers would focus on helping kids understand their unique gifts, talents, strengths and skills with an emphasis on helping them to apply these to a clear career and vocational path. He conveyed his strong dissatisfaction with the current educational system, especially in the universities and colleges, where they were known for indoctrination and poor preparation for kids in the workforce upon graduation.

He recommended that a worldwide committee be developed to create a course curriculum that was modifiable to the certain cultures and faiths, but had a basis of effective outcomes that would ensure the kids would be able to apply discernment, logic, emphasis and training on discovering one's purpose, and how to align their purpose with a gifted-minded service within their community. He continued articulating the importance of educating young minds about appreciating the differences in race, culture, faiths, with an emphasis on not dividing, but to embrace and learn how to collaboratively work together for the common good.

Jacob shared his heartfelt beliefs in the significance of students understanding how to work through conflict resolution while also being trained on how to set goals and develop strategic plans for successful outcomes. He wanted to eliminate much of the unnecessary education that was useless in helping prepare the youth for the future, and instead implement real world applications.

Ultimately, he wanted reform for the entire educational system that focused on kids' strengths, so they could then be guided into their area of specialty through a very unique person-centered type of training. All students would receive the core training of ethics, morality, and lessons learned from history on failed ideology. The course would put a focus on these ideals that worked, and not on those that fell short in this capacity.

After three long days of discussion, it was evident that most were in favor of the ideas Jacob put forth, as they all agreed on developing a committee to spend the next 1-2 years on establishing such a curriculum that would incorporate the best minds in education, religion, history, politics, law, and business, to work in unison. Part of the plan was to have this committee develop the best tools and experts in helping kids and adults fully discover and understand their purpose, and then how to use that to impact the world.

Jacob and the others were extremely excited about the possibility of such a program and its impact on humanity. Also how it would reduce employment, increase economic growth, while improving overall health and wellness. Jacob so eloquently shared his vision of a world where people could live out their unique God-given vision in service to others, and how it would bring communities, and countries together, because its focus would be on working together while bringing a sense of unity, as well as independence.

At the close of the meeting, each of the attendees were going to put a list of those they recommended to be on the committee. Jacob wanted to keep the group fairly small so as to not lose focus on the vision and mission. It was agreed that Jacob would be the final determiner of who would be on the committee.

After three months of applications and interviews, Jacob had his list of twenty one individuals all from different backgrounds and specialties. His committee consisted of the best and brightest in their areas of expertise such as Elon Musk, Michael Jordan, Robert Kiyosaki, Thomas Sowell, Josh Mcdowell, Franklin Graham, Benjamin Netanyahu, the Dalai Lama, father Andrew Greeley, Anthony Robbins, Jack Canfield, Maya Angelou, Robin Williams, Serena Williams, Oprah Winfrey, Carly Fiorina, Condoleezza Rice, Clint Eastwood, Bruce Springsteen, Nancy Reagan, Donald Clifton, Otto Koeger, David Dubois, and David Clutterback.

After the committee was developed, all agreed to meet at least once a month to develop a mentoring curriculum. They decided to split up in groups of three with wide ranges of expertise in different areas. They were commissioned to focus on courses such as critical thinking skills, logic, civics, business and leadership development, debate, conflict resolution, moral education, history, personal growth, multi media, creative arts, entrepreneurship, public speaking, cultural and religious studies, service projects, computer training, music, foreign language, vocational and trade careers. They were also instructed to put a focus on the students' strengths, and interests, as well as set up a core list of courses that would help students to learn the key elements of morality, leadership, decision making, financial management, business mastery and life mastery.

He also stressed his desire to ensure that part of the curriculum was to work with companies to develop job training/paid internship that would lead to employment. Jacob explained to everyone how revolutionary this curriculum was going to be to help prepare and equip them to succeed in life. He further added that he wanted to start with the youth, as they were still forming the ideology and would be more apt to learn, grow and apply it. Eventually they would be developing courses through all stages of life.

The committee met faithfully for two years, after which the curriculum was ready to be presented. Jacob coordinated to present the idea and curriculum to the world at the United Nations, including each of its world leaders. Before doing so, he reconvened with the committee and the original attendees, but this time they met at the Grand Hotel on Mackinaw Island. Jacob was able to reserve the whole island for the event.

It was September 2005, and it was a cool evening with Lake Michigan as its backdrop. Jacob decided to take a stroll before the event and ran into Billy Graham. Both men began speaking about what God had done for them in their calling. Jacob shared the various visions he had over his years and Dr. Graham shared the many visions throughout scripture from Paul, to Daniel, and how God often communicated his will through visions of what he wanted to do for the world, but he needed men and women he could entrust those visions with.

Later that evening Jacob stood up to speak and present his vision and curriculum to the committee. Everyone in attendance knew this was a miracle in the making. They all jokingly stated how refreshing it was that they surprisingly were able to work together considering all the strong personalities between them, like Trump, and others. In the end, everyone gave their blessing on the project.

In his final speech, Jacob informed the others of his vision and why this was so important to him. He shared the pain of going through

World War 2 and the battle of ideology from a global perspective, and reminded all how important it was to properly safeguard and prepare the next generation. Further explaining, "we were only one generation away from possible annihilation at the hands of a maniacal dictator, as in Hitler. He ended on a powerful note: "We must do it for our children."

Once Jacob had the blessing, he prepared to then speak at the United Nations in New York six months later. All the world leaders would be in attendance. Six months later, as Jacob was preparing to take the stage to speak at the United Nations, he met with Dr. Graham and President Bush to pray for what he was going to share. He opened his by thanking the leaders for allowing him to speak at this event. He then proceeded to tell a story of a lesson he had learned from one of the world's greatest leaders, before he was even recognized as a leader, rather, when he was just a child. He proceeded to tell the story of Jesus when his parents lost track of him when he was twelve:

Every year Jesus' parents went to Jerusalem for the Festival of the Passover. [42] When he was twelve years old, they went up to the festival, according to the custom. [43] After the festival was over, while his parents were returning home, the boy Jesus stayed behind in Jerusalem, but they were unaware of it. [44] Thinking he was in their company, they traveled on for a day. Then they began looking for him among their relatives and friends. [45] When they did not find him, they went back to Jerusalem to look for him. [46] After three days they found him in the temple courts, sitting among the teachers, listening to them and asking them questions. [47] Everyone who heard him was amazed at his understanding and his answers. [48] When his parents saw him, they were astonished. His mother said to him, "Son, why have you treated us like this? Your father and I have been anxiously searching for you." [49]And

He said to them, "Why did you seek Me? Did you not know that I must be about My Father's business?"

[a] [50] But they did not understand what he was saying to them.

[51] Then he went down to Nazareth with them and was obedient to them. But his mother treasured all these things in her heart. [52] And Jesus grew in wisdom and stature, and in favor with God and man.

Jacob then began to explain, while linking the story, to why he was there. He recognized how Jesus knew he had a greater calling and purpose in His life, even in His early years. Then as the years progressed, He would live that purpose which would change the world. Jacob admitted that although he knew many of the audience members may not be believers in the Christian faith, that these principles were transferrable, which was his goal by rolling out the world-wide curriculum to the youth.

His goal, and he believed the goals of everyone there, was to make their countries great. He stated that to ensure that goal, each of them had to pour into their youth—the lessons and principles to ensure that. Reminding them all that, "It started with a sense of purpose just as the story of Christ illustrated." While emphasizing, "If we all could help them discover their purpose, calling, while helping them put into action through service and collaboration with others, everybody benefits. Jacob then laid out the plan to everyone, then concluded with promises from Jeremiah and the psalms:

Jacob then laid out the plan to everyone, then ended with promises from Jeremiah.

Jeremiah 29:11–12

"For I know the plans I have for you," declares the LORD, *"plans to prosper you and not to harm you, plans to give you hope and a future. [12] Then you will call on me and come and pray to me, and I will listen to you. [13] You will seek me and find me when you seek me with all your heart. [14] I will be found by you," declares the* LORD,*"*

Jacob stressed that God's desire and plan for his children was to prosper us, not to harm us, and to give us a hope for the future if we would only seek Him. Jacob then shared a passage from psalms 37 written by David to help those in attendance to understand that those who seek the lord and do good would prosper which he stressed was everyone's desire. He reminded them of world history in which they were all aware of those who were defeated and are no more, all because of evil acts. *Psalms 37:*

Do not fret because of those who are evil
or be envious of those who do wrong;
[2] for like the grass they will soon wither,
like green plants they will soon die away.

[3] Trust in the LORD *and do good;*
dwell in the land and enjoy safe pasture.
[4] Take delight in the LORD,
and he will give you the desires of your heart.

⁵ Commit your way to the Lᴏʀᴅ;
trust in him and he will do this:
⁶ He will make your righteous reward shine like the dawn,
your vindication like the noonday sun.

⁷ Be still before the Lᴏʀᴅ
and wait patiently for him;
do not fret when people succeed in their ways,
when they carry out their wicked schemes.

⁸ Refrain from anger and turn from wrath;
do not fret—it leads only to evil.

For those who are evil will be destroyed,
but those who hope in the Lᴏʀᴅ will inherit the land.

¹⁰ A little while, and the wicked will be no more;
though you look for them, they will not be found.
¹¹ But the meek will inherit the land
and enjoy peace and prosperity.

¹² The wicked plot against the righteous
and gnash their teeth at them;
¹³ but the Lord laughs at the wicked,
for he knows their day is coming.

¹⁴ The wicked draw the sword
and bend the bow
to bring down the poor and needy,
to slay those whose ways are upright.
¹⁵ But their swords will pierce their own hearts,
and their bows will be broken.

16 *Better the little that the righteous have*
than the wealth of many wicked;
17 *for the power of the wicked will be broken,*
but the LORD upholds the righteous.

18 *The blameless spend their days under the LORD's care,*
and their inheritance will endure forever.
19 *In times of disaster they will not wither;*
in days of famine they will enjoy plenty.

20 *But the wicked will perish:*
Though the LORD's enemies are like the flowers of the field,
they will be consumed, they will go up in smoke.

21 *The wicked borrow and do not repay,*
but the righteous give generously;
22 *those the LORD blesses will inherit the land,*
but those he curses will be destroyed.

23 *The LORD makes firm the steps*
of the one who delights in him;
24 *though he may stumble, he will not fall,*
for the LORD upholds him with his hand.

25 *I was young and now I am old,*
yet I have never seen the righteous forsaken
or their children begging bread.
26 *They are always generous and lend freely;*
their children will be a blessing.[b]

27 *Turn from evil and do good;*
then you will dwell in the land forever.

28 For the LORD loves the just
and will not forsake his faithful ones.

Wrongdoers will be completely destroyed[c];
the offspring of the wicked will perish.
29 The righteous will inherit the land
and dwell in it forever.

30 The mouths of the righteous utter wisdom,
and their tongues speak what is just.
31 The law of their God is in their hearts;
their feet do not slip.

32 The wicked lie in wait for the righteous,
intent on putting them to death;
33 but the LORD will not leave them in the power of the wicked
or let them be condemned when brought to trial.

34 Hope in the LORD
and keep his way.
He will exalt you to inherit the land;
when the wicked are destroyed, you will see it.

35 I have seen a wicked and ruthless man
flourishing like a luxuriant native tree,
36 but he soon passed away and was no more;
Although I looked for him, he could not be found.

37 Consider the blameless, observe the upright;
a future awaits those who seek peace.[d]
38 But all sinners will be destroyed;
there will be no future[e] for the wicked.

[39] The salvation of the righteous comes from the LORD;
He is their stronghold in times of trouble.
[40] The LORD helps them and delivers them;
he delivers them from the wicked and saves them,
because they take refuge in him.

After sharing the struggles of David in Psalms 37 he closed with the passage from Acts 13:36:

"Now when David had served God's purpose in his own generation, he fell asleep; he was buried with his ancestors and his body decayed."

Jacob stated to the audience, "that each of us was created for a purpose, and that David found His, and lived it out.' Jacob Steele concluded by letting them know his desire was to prepare and equip the youth with the tools needed to find their purpose and to live it out in service to others. The audience erupted in applause as they all internalized his vision. Thereafter, Jacob began implementing the course curriculum, and traveling the world in developing mentoring centers all throughout the globe. Jacob spent the next ten years watching his vision being manifested.

CHAPTER

20

"The Will"

Over the years Jacob spent more time with his grandkids and great grandkids, wanting to ensure he left them a world and a legacy to live up to. He had four kids who were all doing well. Michael was still running Water of Life Industries, but was nearing retirement. Most of Jacob's kin were involved with his company in some capacity, as he always believed in a family-first model, but he never pressured any of them to join. He had helped Michael with bringing on his kids to the company and Michael was training his son Kenneth to take over in the next couple years thereafter. Michael and his wife had 2 children. Jacob's daughter Rachel had married a pilot and they had 2 children as well. Emily married a doctor, and they ended up having 3 children. Jacob's grandson Kevin and his wife Kim supervised the research and development team for Water of Life Europe. Joseph ended up marrying a nurse, and they were committed to working in Latin America running Jacob's foundation. They were the parents of 4 children themselves. Jacob had 11 grandkids and 24 great grandkids.

Family get-togethers were so precious for Jacob. They had a tradition of always getting together as a family at least twice a year during Christmas time and a summer vacation. Of all his grandkids and Great grandkids, Jacob was especially fond of Reece, Elliot, Lane, and Rachel. They adored their great grandpa. He would spend as much time as he could with each of them and was always in attendance at their school events. Reece was 23, Elliot 22, Lane 21, and Rachel 7. Their beloved great grandpa would entertain them with stories of the war, as well as his experiences across the globe on humanitarian affairs. Jacob was concerned about what was going to happen after he was gone. He knew his kids and grandkids all had a strong moral upbringing and would make great decisions, but he wanted to make sure his great grandkids understood what mattered while ensuring they would not make some of the same mistakes he had made. He also wanted to make sure they knew that kindness, compassion, love and service were vital to a successful life. He knew that since they were blessed financially, he wasn't sure how he could help them appreciate the lessons he had learned. He also knew that God had blessed him with a long life and a lot of lessons to pass on to his family.

Jacob was approaching his 89th birthday and was still able to move around quite well, but figured he should go for his annual check up. He soon scheduled a visit to Dr. Thomas who was a long time friend and had blood work done and an overall check up. Two weeks later Dr. Thomas called Jacob and asked him to come in. Jacob went in shortly to meet with the doctor and he expressed concerns about Jacob's bloodwork, and told him that a biopsy would need to be done which was scheduled a week later. After the biopsy Dr. Thomas called Jacob back in and informed Jacob of the issue; Dr. Thomas got right to the point and informed Jacob that he had a very aggressive form of colon cancer and that unfortunately it was not treatable. Dr. Thomas regretfully shared with Jacob that he might have about 6 months left, and it would be best that he moved forward getting his affairs in order. Somehow Jacob was prepared for this, as he knew he already had a full and blessed life.

As Jacob was heading home, he knew he had to let his family, and board of directors know of the news. Jacob first met with his kids and told them all, naturally they all wept at the thought of them " losing" him. To which he reminded them that he lives forever within their hearts and vice versa. They had always admired his courage and faith. He then called a family meeting where he shared the sad news, and they were deeply saddened at the thought of Jacob, aka "Pops," not being around. He then met with his board and his attorney to have the will drawn up.

Jacob spent many hours over the past years deciding on how he wanted to disperse his will before he got called to Heaven. He didn't just want to give the money out, as he knew statistically that money inherited and not earned would be wasted. He decided to issue a certain allotment to each of his kids, leaving his company to Michael and his family with most of the money from investments set in a trust to the grandkids and great grandkids, with clear stipulation of when and how much money would be given. He also left a significant amount in endowment for his foundation and the ongoing work of the mentoring centers in which many of his grandkids were involved, with a sizable salary to continue that work. As for his four great Grandkids he was especially close to, he wanted to make sure he included something special in the will for them. He made it clear to his attorney that they were to complete various tasks/tests that would help prepare them for life and how to handle the amount of money they were to receive. He stressed to his attorney that they were to work together on these tasks in order to help them understand that nothing can be done successfully without others. First, they were to spend time in various career and business endeavors to try and recognize what their passions and interests were. The attorney was to assign a coordinator who would handle all of the projects and scheduling of the activities. The time frames were fluid as Jacob was trying to train and draw out of each of the kids specific talents, and gifts unique to them. He laid out within these tasks that the outcome would be for the kids to discover their purpose, and use it for the good of others. He stated that these tasks would be broken down into the following to bring out the results to discover their Purpose:

1. Discovery of their strengths

2. Discovery of their passions

3. Discovery of their love languages

4. Discovery of their temperaments

5. Discovery of their personality styles and types

6. Discovery of their gifts and talents

7. How to develop a mission, vision and purpose statement

The direction given would detail the activities each would need to complete to get the needed answers, and once they all determined those answers, they would move onto the next task. After all the kids had completed each task to the satisfaction of the coordinator as outlined in the will, they would each be given a key and an allotted amount of money to open up a box for their final project. Once they were able to complete the final project to specific guidelines, they would then receive another key that would open the Inheritance.

After Jacob completed his instructions for the will, he spent the remaining months visiting with friends and family. He traveled as much as his health would allow, to the places around the world where *The Water of Life* plants were based. He wanted to personally thank all those that had made such a difference in the world. He also wanted to go to as many locations as he could where his *Growing Minds* mentoring centers were, to talk with the kids and encourage them to keep their dreams alive. While he traveled, he had a journalist by his side to transcribe his story, and the things Jacob had learned so that he could have a memoir to pass on.

Jacob wanted to make sure he shared those life lessons as he was trying to provide lifelong wisdom to his great grandkids. As his health began to fade, and he was forced to limit his travels, he was looking forward to the upcoming family Christmas visit . He knew it would be his last and nothing made him happier than to be with the ones he loved most. As they finished opening presents and sat down for dinner, Jacob gave a toast and reminded all of them how happy he was to be with everyone this Christmas. He encouraged them to keep this tradition alive, and to always be there for one another.

Shortly after dinner, Jacob retired to his room to rest. As his eyes closed, he fell into a deep sleep and once again, he was back on that all too familiar beach. As he looked around, he saw that same endless amount of people from his original vision, but this time they all were alive and smiling. Leading the group was his old friend Michael, and his lovely Maggie. Jacob was beyond thrilled to see Michael and Maggie, while asking who the others were. Michael and Maggie both told him that they were all the lives he saved and helped from his obedience. As

Jacob wept and was embraced by all, Maggie turned to him and told him it was time to go home.

Michael, his son then went to check on Jacob and when he did, he saw that Dad was gone.

CHAPTER

21

"The Passing of the Torch"

Word spread rapidly at the passing of Jacob Steele. His funeral was scheduled, and was attended by world leaders from all over the globe. Jacob lived a long and beautiful life and passed at the age of 90 on December 25, 2015. All were heartbroken, especially his great grandkids Reece, Elliot, Lane and Rachel. They all sat together at the funeral and went to the casket in unison to say their final goodbyes to their "Pops". After a couple of weeks, the family was called in for the reading of the will with the attorneys involved. At the end of Jacobs life, his assets amounted to over 200 billion dollars. The attorney began with the instructions for the immediate kids and each was allocated what Jacob felt was fair. After most of the will was read and the money was allocated, the attorney directed the four great grandkids to remain and let them know that their "Pops" had special instructions for them. He paused for a moment and opened a keyed box, then pulled out a handwritten letter to the four kids and began reading it to them.

"Dearest Reece, Elliot, Lane and Rachel, if you are hearing these words then I am now gone to be with Jesus and grandma Maggie. I want you all to know how much "Pops" loves you and misses you. I left something super special for you, as I know how much each of you love games, so I have put together some tests/challenges for you all to complete together and when you've done that then you will receive your inheritance. I have left detailed instructions with my attorney and Ms. Roy, the coordinator on the various tasks you are to complete to her satisfaction before moving onto the next assignment. I am doing this because I want more than anything for all of you to learn and discover your purpose in life without having to go through all the struggles and mistakes I endured to discover mine. I also want to make sure you understand your purpose is God-given and must be used to serve others. I wanted to ensure each of you learns the valuable lessons in life to be good stewards for what has been given to you. Make sure you help and support one another and know that together with God's help you can do anything. I want to share a valuable story that your great great grandmother shared with me from the bible.

The Parable of the Talents

[14] *"For it will be like a man going on a journey, who called his servants[a] and entrusted to them his property. [15] To one he gave five talents,[b] to another two, to another one, to each according to his ability. Then he went away. [16] He who had received the five talents went at once and traded with them, and he made five talents more. [17] So also he who had the two talents made two talents more. [18] But he who had received the one talent went and dug in the ground and hid his master's money. [19] Now after a long time the master of those servants came and settled accounts with them. [20] And he who had received the five talents came forward, bringing five talents more, saying, 'Master, you*

delivered to me five talents; here, I have made five talents more.' [21] His master said to him, 'Well done, good and faithful servant.[c] You have been faithful over a little; I will set you over much. Enter into the joy of your master.' [22] And he also who had the two talents came forward, saying, 'Master, you delivered to me two talents; here, I have made two talents more.' [23] His master said to him, 'Well done, good and faithful servant. You have been faithful over a little; I will set you over much. Enter into the joy of your master.' [24] He also who had received the one talent came forward, saying, 'Master, I knew you to be a hard man, reaping where you did not sow, and gathering where you scattered no seed, [25] so I was afraid, and I went and hid your talent in the ground. Here, you have what is yours.' [26] But his master answered him, 'You wicked and slothful servant! You knew that I reap where I have not sown and gather where I scattered no seed? [27] Then you ought to have invested my money with the bankers, and at my coming I should have received what was my own with interest. [28] So take the talent from him and give it to him who has the ten talents. [29] For to everyone who has will more be given, and he will have an abundance. But from the one who has not, even what he has will be taken away. [30] And cast the worthless servant into the outer darkness. In that place there will be weeping and gnashing of teeth.'

Jacob continued in his letter that if they successfully complete the tests they will discover their "talents," and if they share them with others through service, then they will be successful and make the world a better place and make "Pops" extremely proud. Jacob ended the letter stating he believed in each of them and he would be praying for them and couldn't wait to see them some day."

The attorney then read the instructions to the kids with Ms. Roy and wished the kids good luck. Over the next year, the kids were faithful in following the instructions to the very last detail. Over that year, the kids discovered their passions, strengths, love language, temperament, personality style, personality type, gifts/talents, spiritual blessings. Ms. Roy had them take numerous tests and assessments to help them better understand how God created them. Once they all had learned to work together and knew their purpose to Ms. Roy's satisfaction, they were each given a key and a box. They all gathered together to open their boxes and each was given an envelope and instructions. The envelopes had $100,000 and instructions specific to their purpose in service to others. They were also instructed to work together and use the money given their specific gifts/talents and purpose to help the assigned group they had worked with over the last year that would most benefit. Ms. Roy used an illustration from scripture to help explain from I Corinthians 12

"4 There are different kinds of gifts, but the same Spirit distributes them. 5 There are different kinds of service, but the same Lord. 6 There are different kinds of working, but in all of them and in everyone it is the same God at work.

7 Now to each one the manifestation of the Spirit is given for the common good. 8 To one there is given through the Spirit a message of wisdom, to another a message of knowledge by means of the same Spirit, 9 to another faith by the same Spirit, to another gifts of healing by that one Spirit, 10 to another miraculous powers, to another prophecy, to another distinguishing between spirits, to another speaking in different kinds of tongues,[a] and to still another the interpretation of tongues. [b] 11 All these are the work of one and the same Spirit, and he distributes them to each one, just as he determines.

[12] Just as a body, though one, has many parts, but all its many parts form one body, so it is with Christ. [13] For we were all baptized by[c] one Spirit so as to form one body—whether Jews or Gentiles, slave or free—and we were all given the one Spirit to drink. [14] Even so the body is not made up of one part but of many.

[15] Now if the foot should say, "Because I am not a hand, I do not belong to the body," it would not for that reason stop being part of the body. [16] And if the ear should say, "Because I am not an eye, I do not belong to the body," it would not for that reason stop being part of the body. [17] If the whole body were an eye, where would the sense of hearing be? If the whole body were an ear, where would the sense of smell be? [18] But in fact God has placed the parts in the body, every one of them, just as he wanted them to be. [19] If they were all one part, where would the body be? [20] As it is, there are many parts, but one body.

[21] The eye cannot say to the hand, "I don't need you!" And the head cannot say to the feet, "I don't need you!" [22] On the contrary, those parts of the body that seem to be weaker are indispensable, [23] and the parts that we think are less honorable we treat with special honor. And the parts that are unpresentable are treated with special modesty, [24] while our presentable parts need no special treatment. But God has put the body together, giving greater honor to the parts that lacked it, [25] so that there should be no division in the body, but that its parts should have equal concern for each other. [26] If one part suffers, every part suffers with it; if one part is honored, every part rejoices with it.

[27] Now you are the body of Christ, and each one of you is a part of it. [28] And God has placed in the church first of all apostles, second prophets, third teachers, then miracles, then gifts of healing, of helping, of guidance, and of different kinds of tongues. [29] Are all apostles? Are all prophets? Are all teachers? Do all work miracles? [30] Do all have gifts of healing? Do all speak in tongues[d]? Do all interpret? [31] Now eagerly desire the greater gifts.

Ms. Roy instructed the kids to learn what the scripture was teaching–that we are all different, but God uses our differences so we can work together to make a bigger difference. The kids decided to combine their money and use their gifts to help support efforts down in Guatemala to help support a school k-12 to ensure kids had a great education, food, clothing, and assisted in developing medical clinics and vocational training programs. They spent that next year ensuring they oversaw the success of the program. Upon their return they met with the board of the foundation and gave their report. After the board meeting, the Attorney and Ms. Roy met with them and gave each of the kids another key and one box. This key was different and the attorney instructed the kids by telling them that this key was a puzzle and that they had 15 minutes to figure it out. Given the kids knew their gifts and talents they each contributed to solving the puzzle and they were able to combine the four keys into one and successfully open the box. In the box was another letter from "Pops".

"In the letter Jacob congratulated the kids on their great work in discovering their purpose and more importantly learning how to work together. He told them that because they were faithful on this scale, then they would be given much more." The attorney then handed the kids each a check. In total their inheritance was $50 billion. Ms. Roy continued reading the rest of the letter to the kids. Jacob stated that with that money they could do pretty much anything they wanted but he asked them to take the lessons they had learned and apply them to their lives in service and good for those in greatest need. He closed by telling them he loved them and knew they would make the right decision."

All the kids looked at one another and decided to follow their wise Pops' advice and be good stewards while figuring out how they could use the money for good, purposeful, impactful ways just as Pop's did during his lifetime. As they said goodbye to the attorney and Ms. Roy, they could almost hear Pops laughing in joy.

ABOUT THE AUTHOR

Born in Carbondale, Illinois, to George and Dolores Peters and the youngest of six, I grew up in the Chicago suburbs while our mother supported the family largely on her own due to my fathers incarceration. Academics didn't come easily, so I channeled my energy into gymnastics at Homewood-Flossmoor High School and began an eight-year military career. I retired from the Army as a First Lieutenant, where I learned the discipline and structure that later helped me pursue a psychology degree from the University of Illinois. Those years laid a solid foundation and led me to study philosophy at Southern Evangelical Seminary and to undertake seminary work. Those leadership lessons carried over into chaplaincy in a New York jail, where I ministered to many inmates.

Today I'm happily married and residing in Frisco, Texas, with five wonderful children who fill our world with joy. Covenant Case Management Services, based in North Carolina, is my company and the vehicle for serving individuals with intellectual disabilities, mental health challenges, and substance use disorders. The Nehemiah Project Covenant of Love, a nonprofit I founded, serves homelessness, veterans, seniors, those battling addiction, individuals with mental health or developmental disabilities, at-risk youth, and abused women.

The network extends its reach in North Carolina and Central America.

To strengthen collaboration with other nonprofits and spread the Nehemiah message worldwide, I launched the Nehemiah International Foundation Growing Minds Mentoring Center that helps at-risk youth discover purpose and supports families in building strong foundations for their children.

As a bestselling author, I've published four books, with the fifth "The Inheritance" slated for December 2025 and a sixth manuscript already underway. On Purpose with Paul, my television show, airs Mondays at 7 pm Central on Nowmedia.com and reaches millions. I also serve as an executive producer with Abundance Studios where we partner together to create life impacting documentaries and partner with Celebrity Branding as a bestselling author.

My passions include reading, mentoring, continual self-improvement, serving others, traveling, and helping people discover their life purpose. I aim to live each day fully and leave a positive imprint on everyone I meet.